'Pierce delivers some masterful narrative which will hold children aged 10 and upwards enthralled.' *Evening Echo*

'I was captivated by the writing and I couldn't put it down ... It is obviously a challenge to be able to make vivid and compelling a story whose ending we all know but Pierce manages this ... writing is entirely captivating, the detail fascinating and the terror real.' *NI4Kids*

'A stunning debut ... beautifully-written, exciting book' *Verbal Magazine*

'Beautifully handled ... beautifully written ... I enjoyed it very, very much.' *BBC Radio Arts Extra*

'This breathtaking book takes you on the deck of the *Titanic* with its amazing descriptive language ... I would recommend this book to anybody who enjoys reading a spooky, emotional book and is interested in the fascinating events of 1912. I would rate this book 10/10.' *Guardian Children's Books Online*

Tallaght-born Nicola Pierce is a writer who splits her life between Drogheda and Belfast. *Spirit of the Titanic* is her first book for children.

Spirit of the Titanic

Nicola Pierce

THE O'BRIEN PRESS
DUBLIN

'For Damian'

First published 2011 by The O'Brien Press Ltd,
12 Terenure Road East, Rathgar, Dublin 6, Ireland.
Tel: +353 1 4923333; Fax: +353 1 4922777
E-mail: books@obrien.ie
Website: www.obrien.ie
Reprinted 2011 (twice), 2012.

ISBN: 978-1-84717-190-0

British Library Cataloguing-in-publication Data
A catalogue record for this title is available from the British Library

4 5 6 7 8 9 10
12 13 14 15 16

Cover image: Dave Hopkins
Interior illustration by Emma Byrne
Printed by CPI Cox and Wyman Ltd.
The paper in this book is produced using pulp from managed forests.

The O'Brien Press receives
assistance from

Prologue

The twentieth of April 1910 is a day that I can never forget. The only thing I can't remember is exactly what day it was. It definitely wasn't a Sunday because that was my only day off from my job at Harland & Wolff's shipyard in Belfast. And it wasn't a Saturday either, or else I would have finished in the early afternoon, as Saturdays were just half-days. Saturday was also the day we got paid, when the line out the door of the accounts office was longer than the massive ship I was helping to build.

Nevertheless, I remember everything else about that day. For instance, I got up, as usual, at a quarter to six and put back on the clothes I had worn the previous day, which I left on the floor beside my bed, ready and waiting to be picked up again. After that, I made my way, quietly as possible, so as not to disturb my mother, down to the kitchen, stretching my legs to overstep the creakiest part of the stairs.

On winter mornings I needed to light a candle and even put on my old jacket because downstairs was always so chilly at that hour. Fortunately, the mornings were a lot brighter in April. On the whole, I didn't mind the early start, though even I had to admit it was easier to get up when the sun was already in the sky and the birds were singing loudly and, so it seemed to me, much more cheerfully than in December or January.

In the kitchen I threw cold water over my face and dried it with the tea towel, something I only did when it was safe to do so. Then I cut myself a thick slice of bread, carelessly covered it with jam and began to eat as I took the lunch my mother left for me, jamming it into my jacket pocket. Her never-ending sadness over my father's death, along with her constant dislike of me, didn't stop her from making the cheese sandwich. In fact, it meant a lot more to me than I realised at the time, that she continued to make it; that and washing my work clothes on Saturday evenings, after I went to bed, were the only things she did for me now.

I left the house still chewing on my bread. It seemed important to both of us that I be gone before she got up for her factory job. To be honest, it was a relief to shut the door behind me and join the crowd of workers heading in the same direction, to the shipyard, where I could forget about my mother's unyielding gloom and my sometimes utter loneliness for the family we used to be with Da.

Three years had passed since he died and I already felt a whole lifetime older than the child I used to be. He had gone fishing in a storm, with his friend, Daniel, in a flimsy rowing boat that must have completely collapsed under the battering of waves and angry winds. Nothing was ever found, at any rate, of either the little boat or its two passengers.

At fifteen years of age I was one of the youngest of this army of employees and maybe I was one of the proudest too. It was Da's brother, my Uncle Albert, who got me the job. He was one of the draughtsmen and spent his day in a huge, open room, standing over the longest desk I've ever seen. It was here that the ships we built were first sketched out with all the complicated mathematics and line-drawing. Uncle Al would tell me that he hoped one day to be able to send me to college, to learn his trade, but I much preferred working on the ships themselves, being up close to them as they took shape in front of me.

That morning, just like any other, I kept my eyes focused over the roofs of the neighbours' houses for my first glimpse of *Titanic*. I couldn't help it; every time I caught sight of her my heart would jump just a little. She wasn't alone; on her right sat her sister, the *Olympic*, who was the older of the two, work having started on her a few months earlier. Therefore, she looked liked a proper ship, while *Titanic* was mostly still a skeleton, with just the bare bones, ribs, clavicle and femurs on show. But *Titanic* would be the greater one: the biggest, heaviest, most expensive ship ever to be built in the whole world. As Charlie, my boss, would say, 'We're making history, boys, imagine that!'

The nearer I got to the shipyard, the larger the crowd grew. Something like twenty thousand men worked at the yard, though not all at the same time. I worked the day shift with Charlie and the others, while at night you could see the hundreds of torches swarming all over the two ships as the night shift took over.

'Sammy, over here! Look at him, Ed; he's the only lad I know who smiles his way to work.' Charlie's curly black hair was sticking out at all angles from beneath his dirty soft cap, which was always pushed that far away from his forehead it was a wonder it never slid off – reminding me of how my father used to wear his.

'Aye, well it's a lot better than having to look at your miserable mug of a morning.' Ed always had something smart to say, no matter how early it was.

This was a typical greeting from my workmates. They were the two riveters in our squad and I was their catch-boy. The riveters were the kings of the shipyard and one day I hoped, to Uncle Al's mild disappointment, to be just like them. It wasn't an easy job and I suppose there was plenty of truth to Al's warning that I'd be 'as deaf as a lamp-post by the time you're twenty-five.'

Jack, always the last to arrive, was the heater-boy. Two years older than me, he was the most unambitious person I had ever met, but he was also one of the most likeable. He sidled up to us, a lazy grin on his broad freckled face, hands in pockets.

'Mornin' all!'

Ed nagged him mercilessly, doing his utmost to unsettle Jack's yawning self-confidence, 'Hmpphh! Afternoon, more like. What happened this time? You couldn't eat your kippers fast enough or maybe your butler overslept?'

Jack, who was never serious about anything, was more than happy to answer Ed's silly questions: 'If you must know, I had to escort a very nice girl to her place of work.'

As usual, Ed refused to let him have the last word, 'Well, from now on have her escort you here instead.'

We joined the thousands that stood outside the shipyard's green gates. It was Ed who decided that we met early before the gates were unlocked at 6.20am. He had never forgiven Jack for arriving too late, one morning, to get inside the gates before they closed at 6.35am. Jack had to wait outside on the street, until 7.30am, which was the next time they opened. This meant that he lost an hour's pay for himself and probably for the rest of the squad as I ended up doing both his job and mine. Of course, this slowed us down and fewer rivets could be hammered into place and since we got paid per rivet every single second mattered.

The rivets are like big, stubby nails that bolt down the sheets of steel all over the outside of a ship's body. Charlie loved to explain what we did in one short sentence, 'It's us who put the flesh on her.' Before the rivets were handed over by me, to be hammered into place, they had to be heated to the right temperature. Jack's job was to pluck the rivet out of the fire, using his tongs, only when it was a certain shade of cherry-red, and roll it down the chute, to where I was waiting. Snatching it up with my own tongs, I would sprint as hard as I could, presenting the inflamed rivet to Ed and Charlie, whether they were on the ground beside me, or sixty feet up in the air.

On that April morning they took their places way up the side of the ship, as *Titanic*'s underbelly had already been coated over with steel. I'm sure I was very fit from all the running and climbing I did. Since the spring weather remained calm and sunny, I didn't have to worry about the wind catching me unawares half-way up the ladder, trying to knock me off my balance or the tongs out of my sweaty grasp.

Both the night and day shifts were made up of dozens upon dozens of rivet squads. I imagined that the noise of the constant battering against the rivet heads, from a thousand different hammers, could be heard for miles around Belfast, and maybe even miles out to sea. Now, that was something to consider. How far out could the banging be heard? The terrific noise was why so many riveters went deaf in later years.

That afternoon, during our lunch-break, I asked Charlie if he thought the hammering could be heard as far as the coast of England, which I knew wasn't too far away, on the other side of the Irish Sea.

'Aye, surely, and those who hear it probably think it's the sound of church bells on the wind.'

Not one of us in the squad had ever been to sea. It didn't seem fair that we would make these ships with our bare hands but never get to sail on them once we were finished.

Many a Sunday I spent staring out beyond Belfast Lough, wondering what it would be like to be completely free of land, and to be standing, instead, on a grand floating island that moved from one side of the world to the other. Imagine that. Everywhere you look, no matter what side you are on, all you can see is water and more water. I wanted to know if the sky and sea ever met. When I stood down at the docks and looked out into the distance, I could just about convince myself that they did.

'What in God's name is he daydreaming about now?'

growled Ed. He was pulling on his after-lunch fag and staring at me in exasperation, making Charlie laugh and Jack's grin even wider than usual. They all waited expectantly while I blushed the perfect shade of cherry-red, I'm sure.

Shyly, I shrugged my shoulders and offered up my thoughts to them, 'I was just thinking, wouldn't it be lovely to be able to go with her when she leaves?'

Only Charlie knew who I was talking about. Ed, however, got the wrong end of the stick and was a little shocked. 'What? You have a girlfriend already and you didn't tell us? You're a bit too young to be getting so serious, don't you think?'

Jack added his bit, more than likely just to annoy Ed, 'If he's big enough, he's old enough.'

'No, no, I meant *her*.' I pointed to *Titanic*, causing Jack to roll his eyes towards the sky. Ignoring him, I turned to the older men, to plead my case, 'Wouldn't you like to leave here, just for a while, and see the world from such a magnificent ship, and get a look at the passengers, to see where they're going and why?'

Both men took a second or two to think about this and then they both nodded, although Ed was quick to say, 'Just for a while, mind. Belfast will always be home to me.'

Charlie was typically more expansive.

'Imagine going first class; it would be like living all day, every day, in the best hotel in the world. I've always fancied seeing America myself. Is that where you'd like to sail to, Sammy, take in the bright lights and tall buildings of New York City?'

'Maybe. I suppose, but I also think I'd be happy enough to just stay onboard her for the rest of my life and never have to live in a house again.'

Ed stubbed out his fag as the buzzer sounded out for us to return to work. 'Daft bugger! Just be careful what you wish for, hey? That sounds a bit silly to me.'

We packed up our things and headed back to our individual posts. Ed couldn't resist bellowing a last instruction to me before he and Charlie began to climb the ladder, 'Just keep those rivets coming and maybe you'll make us all rich enough to come with you on your lifelong voyage. Ha! Ha!'

Ed always laughed louder than anyone else at his own jokes. In fact, he didn't care if nobody else laughed at all.

'You should never tell him anything important' was Jack's parting shot as he headed off in the direction of his furnace.

The next couple of hours passed quickly enough. I tried my best to keep count of how many rivets I delivered but, as usual, I lost count after twelve or so. I did have a strange moment when I was coming back down the ladder, in the late afternoon. I thought someone was calling for help, but I must have imagined it. It would have been impossible. Even if somebody was hurt – and I did take a few precious seconds to look around me, but could only see men and boys hard at work – there is no way I would have been able to hear them. I forgot about it as soon the next boiling rivet rolled down to be collected.

Ed and Charlie were moving farther and farther up the ship and they both look pleased with our performance rate. I picked up the rivet, with the tongs, and ran to the foot of the ladder. The sweat was running down my back, causing, at least, a certain coolness as long as I kept moving. It was only when I was standing still that the heat was suffocating. As I climbed, a flash of movement or colour caught my eye. A dog? I was quite high up; maybe it was just a rat in the ship's belly. We had to chase them off from time to time, rats the size of small dogs, although they would rarely show themselves this late in the day. Ach, it was nothing. The heat must be getting to me; I would ask Charlie for a quick mouthful from the bottle of water he kept at his side.

Suddenly I heard barking as clearly as if a dog was at my feet. I stopped climbing, to catch my breath. The barking was loud and frantic, confusing me as I watched only men alongside me, beneath me and above me. Where on earth was it coming from? My heart was pounding from all the exercise and from something else as I became aware of the distance between me and the ground. For the first time I felt a little queasy at the sight. It made me feel cold and shivery, as if I was coming down with the dreaded flu.

I longed to scream at the invisible dog to shut up. Then again, maybe the barking was inside my head. One thing was certain; I needed to get off this blasted ladder, and I needed both hands to do so. I let go of my tongs, allowing it and the glowing rivet to crash below and began to creep downwards, shutting my eyes in a drastic effort to calm myself, feeling for the step below me with my trembling foot. However, my hands were clammy, even wet, and I couldn't, wouldn't trust them to keep me safe so I brought my foot back to the original position, with some relief. I was stuck, once more, unable to move up or down.

The only thing I could think to do was call for help. Clinging blindly to the ladder, I shouted out, praying that someone would notice me. Only I couldn't hear my voice, instead I heard a whole lot of other calls for help. Babies were crying, not one but hundreds. What was happening to me? The dog kept barking and all these voices were swirling around and around me, making me dizzy; *help us, please help us, somebody help us.*

'Oh, my God! Samuel?'

It was Charlie, sounding absolutely horrified. I don't know

how I managed to hear him. Although it occurred to me that he wasn't as far away as I thought. Keeping my eyes closed, I could only call back his name for an answer, 'Charlie.'

'Okay, pet, you're okay. Just open your eyes and look at me. Can you do that? Just concentrate on me, nothing else.'

I wanted to do just as he told me to. In fact, I opened my eyes to do just that, to gaze upon his grimy face and greasy hair. Only when I looked up to see him, I found that he was surrounded by a dense crowd of men, women and children. Their faces were so white that they were transparent and I could only make out dark circles in place of eyes and mouths. Some of the men seemed to be wearing top hats, while most of the women were poorly dressed, their hair all askew. I could see right through them, to the far side of the gantry. They had no legs, so they seemed to hang still in mid-air. Hundreds and hundreds of them – ghosts, phantoms, ghouls – whatever they were, they were horrible, terrifying me with their silent stares. It was perhaps to get away from them as far and as fast as possible that I instinctively let go of the ladder. And it worked, their empty staring faces got further and further away from me and I hardly noticed Charlie's scream. 'Nooo!'

That calm, sunny day is one I'll always remember and can never forget because the twentieth of April, in the year 1910, was the day that I, Samuel Joseph Scott, died.

Chapter One

My wish had come true. How I longed to be able to share my news with Ed, Charlie and Jack but I couldn't. The three of them stood side by side with David, my replacement, in the crowd, as *Titanic* prepared to pull away from Belfast to begin her maiden voyage. It was all very thrilling and I found myself much carried away by the party atmosphere onboard and on the docks below, waving gaily along with everyone else, in spite of myself, but, of course, my friends could neither see nor hear me. Nobody could.

The world hadn't ended or even changed much since I smashed up my skull that day, though Charlie's dark hair went grey in the weeks after my fall. He was the only one to look properly sad, telling Ed that he blamed himself for not coming down the ladder to grab a hold of me.

Ed was his usual practical self. 'You can't say that, Charlie. No way. It wasn't your fault. If you had reached him, he might've taken you with him. It was just one of those things. When your time is up, that's it!'

Charlie didn't sound comforted by this. His voice wavered as he tried to get Ed to understand. 'But you didn't see his face, Ed. He was scared, more than scared; it was like he could see something dreadful. He called out to me and I did nothing, absolutely nothing.'

Ed refused to be drawn any further. He kept it to himself that he felt I had simply been daydreaming as usual and missed my footing; he didn't want to fall out with his friend.

I was quickly replaced by a skinny sixteen-year-old who was no way near as fast as I was. On his first day Ed nobly held his tongue while Charlie coldly informed a bewildered-looking David that he had 'big shoes to fill'. After that, Charlie's only conversation with the boy was to shout at him, from time to time, 'Watch your bloody step, why don't you!'

Within a week or two the others returned to their usual ways. Ed went back to his jovial bullying of Jack who smilingly refused to be moved one way or the other. The four of them continued to meet every morning before the gates opened and then, once over the threshold, they made their way to where I was waiting for them, to watch them at their day's work.

I wanted to tell Charlie that I was okay, that he shouldn't

feel sad for me, but I couldn't. I mean, I tried talking to him, whispering directly into his ear, but he could never hear me. Once or twice, however, he would stop what he was doing to look slowly about him, as if, perhaps, sensing I was there. This made Ed very nervous and the older man had to fight the urge to shout at Charlie to keep hammering.

Since Da's death Charlie was the only person that really listened to me when I said something, even something daft, and I did find it hard, in the beginning, to appreciate that he could no longer hear me now. It took a bit of getting used to, though perhaps not as much as you might think. To be honest, I didn't feel too sad over my ghostly state, if that's what I was. In some ways it wasn't too different from the life I had led before I started working here, when nobody had taken much notice of me anyway. So I didn't feel particularly lonely. What I did miss, however, was feeling that I mattered to someone. Da was lost to me and now I was lost to Charlie, but at least I could still enjoy his company, Monday to Saturday.

We continued to have our lunch together every day, same as always, only I had to do without my cheese sandwich and nobody knew I was sitting alongside them, listening to the gossip and laughing at Ed's rotten jokes.

In this way I learned many different things, like, for instance, Ed's daily silent disappointment with his wife's sandwiches that were either scrambled or fried egg between chunky slices of bread. He didn't like egg but wouldn't risk hurting her feelings by saying so. It was quite a revelation to find he had a soft side for someone else's feelings.

Charlie longed to take out his library book and read it as he ate, and he often wished he could find somewhere quiet to eat his lunch, away from the demands of Ed with his constant need to be to the expert on every subject.

Meanwhile, Jack spent a lot of his time thinking about the girl who sold him his cigarettes at the corner shop. He could never be sure if she really liked him or not.

I wasn't terribly interested in David. If anything, I was jealous of him for taking my place and enjoyed finding fault with his work rather than learning more about him.

It wasn't that I could read their minds or hear the voices in their heads, it was more than I could sense what they were feeling and maybe it helped that I knew them before the fall. At night I maintained my supervision of the building of *Titanic*, hovering over the shoulders of the evening crew, none of whom was familiar to me. It was a peculiar thing to hear the more sensitive ones complain of feeling they were being watched.

As it turned out, I wasn't the only one to die on the ship. I watched a boy about my age end up like me, fractured skull and legs broken beneath his crumpled body. A year after the young lad's accident, his father, who was a rivet-counter, was counting away, fifty feet from the ground, balancing on flimsy scaffolding. I sensed what was going to happen and tried my best to warn the man, but he ignored the chill he might've felt on the back of his neck. Mourning his son was taking up all his energy, so that once he started counting he was completely switched off from any distraction or sensation. Sure enough, he imitated exactly his son's passing. As with the boy, I saw his spirit leave his body; a light mist exited from his gaping mouth and flew upwards until I could see it no more.

Why I was here, I didn't know. Why I hadn't yet met my father or God or my mother's parents who had been dead for years was mystifying. Nothing was how I'd expected it to be. To be sure, I was glad to be in a familiar – as well as my favourite – place in the whole world, still surrounded by my friends and colleagues. Nevertheless I did worry, from time to time, that I was lost or had been forgotten about.

And then there was the conversation that I heard one winter's morning. I recognised the man as someone my father used to say hello to; he lived on the street behind us and was also a riveter. Peering out at Ed and Charlie, from beneath the drenched peak of his cap, he nodded to them as he approached. 'Aren't you the ones that young lad worked with, the Scott boy?'

His temper soured by the wet weather, Ed's reply was

blunt and careless, 'What of it?'

Obviously expecting a better show of interest, the man was taken aback with the unfriendly reception. 'Oh. Well. I just thought you'd want to know that his mother died last night.'

Ed shrugged and turned away, pretending he hadn't looked at Charlie to see his reaction. Not that there was much to be seen. 'Thanks, mate,' was all Charlie said, before stepping onto the ladder. I followed him and that was that. Maybe she was happy now. I hoped so. It didn't seem right to feel nothing more than, well, nothing more than this, but I suppose she had sort of given up or, or died, the day she heard about Da. And I spent the next three years missing her, there and then, when she was standing right in front of me. So I had nothing more now to give.

Aside from the waving and the cheering, there was a certain amount of sadness in the air as *Titanic* bid farewell to Belfast. Most of the men who had worked on her had come to see her off and mixed in with their pride at what they had produced was just a little bit of sorrow at having to say goodbye to her. For the last two years she had been part of the landscape of Belfast. I certainly wasn't the only one who enjoyed looking for her at every opportunity. Her progression from bare skeleton, to empty ship, to her present magnificence had been watched, and shared, by the locals, near and far. Wasn't I the lucky one then?

All around me was the staff of *Titanic*, the new crew who had taken over from the draughtsmen, the riveters, carpenters, painters and electricians. It was their turn now to tend to the ship. They were the maids, the stewards, the chefs and, of course, the sailors. Nobody said anything, but I felt it keenly as the thousand-strong crowd, in their crisp new uniforms, looked out over the railings at the men who had built her; I was sure I heard the collective feeling, 'She's ours now.'

As the ship's horn sounded out its final farewell I experienced a ferocious wrench and I realised that this was it; I was leaving Belfast at long last. From now on everything was going to be different, except for dear *Titanic*. I felt bound to her alone. Like a parent I had watched over her birth and like my child she had to outlive my death. If I wasn't going to heaven, then I was happy to stay with her forevermore, though it would have been more perfect if Charlie could have come too.

'Da, are we going to America now?' The little boy was tugging excitedly on his father's jacket with one hand as he continued to wave the other at the crowd.

'Not yet, Joseph. Remember what I told you. We have to collect lots more passengers in England, France and County Cork and then we're on our way.'

Goodness! It was the man from the street behind us, the one who brought the news about my mother. What was he doing here? That must be his wife with the baby girl, while

Joseph looked to be no more than six or seven. How small they looked, dwarfed by the large crowd of efficient staff and the overall brilliance of the ship.

His wife spoke in hushed tones, 'Let's find our room, Jim, I can't wait to see it.'

'Alright, if everyone is sure that they've finished saying goodbye to poor Belfast?'

His wife's excited smile was tinged with a bitter sweetness. 'I think it's Belfast that has finished saying goodbye to poor us,' she murmured.

Jim held her gaze for a second or two and a feeling of something powerful passed between them. I was fascinated. Then he bent down to pick up the suitcase at his feet, take Joseph by the hand, and declare cheerfully, 'Come on, then. Let's go find where we'll be living for the next few days.'

As I watched them head off, I determined to meet up with them later – once I had taken my fill of the sight. I felt a lot happier in myself. There was something about Jim that reminded me of Charlie, who, in turn, had always reminded me a little of my father. He shared his sureness and solid sense of self. There was nothing to hide, only things to protect.

⚜ ⚜ ⚜

Da and I used to walk for miles on the days when my mother's moods were particularly bad. When she wasn't so bad, he used to take her out for walks instead. Naturally I preferred when it was him and me. One day he told me a story about something that had happened when I was a little baby, promising me it was absolutely true. Ma was giving me a bottle when there was a knock on the door. As the door was unlocked and she didn't want to disturb me, she called out to whoever it was to come in. It was a handsome woman, a gypsy, wearing layers of colourful clothes with lots of noisy bracelets and earrings that cracked against one another as she strode into our tiny kitchen.

'Good morning, missus. I was wondering if you'd spare a bit of bread or a few pence?'

My mother was flustered and told her she had no money to give.

'But, perhaps, you'd have some bread for me? I've five hungry mouths at home and no husband to help me.'

Feeling slightly trapped, Ma was determined, however, not to let the strange woman go through her presses. The faster she gave her some food, the quicker the visit would be over. But what was she to do about me? I continued to feed hungrily, gulping down the milk I had been crying for all morning. The woman, seeing my mother's predicament, shot over to her. 'Please, let me hold the child, don't take the bottle from him.'

With some reluctance my mother placed me in the gypsy's

25

fleshy arms, hoping that the constant rattle of the jewellery wouldn't frighten me.

'Ooh, what a beauty!'

Here my father hunched up his shoulders and put on a dreadful high-pitched voice with plenty of hysterical cackles. He sounded like a mad old witch, making me laugh out loud and completely doubt whether any of this actually took place. Anyway, the story went that when my mother returned with the bread the woman was looking at me rather strangely. Ma panicked and reached for me instantly. 'What's wrong, is he alright?'

The woman didn't hand me over immediately. Instead she asked Ma what my name was. Wishing that she was brave enough to snatch me out of the gypsy's arms, Ma could only answer her obediently, 'Samuel.'

'Aha! "God's chosen one".' The woman nodded her head slowly, as if in complete agreement with whatever she was thinking to herself. 'That's what Samuel means, and it's a fine name, for one like him.'

Ma was suddenly intrigued. 'What do you mean, "one like him"?'

'This one is special. I can see the wisdom in his eyes as he stares directly into mine. He has been here before, many, many times.'

My mother, who hardly believed in anything outside of

what she could physically touch, was impressed, nonetheless, by the woman's obvious reverence.

The gypsy continued to talk, almost to herself, as she gazed upon me in my state of blissful ignorance, 'Yes, yes. He may have a long life or he may have a short one, but that's not what's important. It's what he's going to do. There's a reason for his being here. I can't tell you any more than that.'

❖ ❖ ❖

There is another story too, my father only ever told it to me the one time and we never mentioned it again. I felt he was hoping for me to enlighten him in some way, but I couldn't remember a single thing about this episode. I was only three at the time. He woke up one night to hear me chatting away in my bedroom, with lots of giggling and even some lines of a nursery rhyme that I knew. Convinced that someone had broken in and was planning to kidnap me, he couldn't get to me fast enough. To his relief, I was quite alone and utterly delighted to see him.

'Dada! You play with me?'

'It's night-time, Samuel. You have to go asleep now.'

Apparently I agreed with him readily enough, explaining that, 'Grampie Peter says I have to be a good boy.'

Peter was the name of my mother's father who had died when I was a few months old.

✤ ✤ ✤

Jim and his family were down below in their cabin, in steerage, the location of the third-class cabins, thoroughly enjoying themselves. His wife had tears in her eyes as she took in the freshly painted walls and the brand new furniture. Jim and Joseph watched her indulgently while the baby slept through all the fuss, including the heavy thud-thud of the ship's engines.

'Oh, my, I've never seen anything like it. I just can't believe it. Even the sheets and the pillows are brand new, just for us.'

Jim took the baby from her, so that she could inspect the linen more closely. Like me, he was more familiar with the ship thanks to his helping to build her.

'And this is only where we sleep. There's also a huge dining room and then there's a sort of common room where the children can play and we can meet other people like us who are setting out for a new life. You never know, Isobel, we might make some friends who could become our neighbours in America.'

His wife beamed at him. 'I have a good feeling about this now. I was so nervous about leaving Ireland for God knows what, but this marvellous ship has put my mind at ease. I think it's a sign that we're definitely doing the right thing.'

Chapter Two

How I longed to feel the wind on my face. I only understand now that it's the small, seemingly insignificant events – wind blowing through your hair, lifting it in uneven tufts or every pore on your body opening up to that first warmth of the morning's sun – that makes a person feel truly alive. Sometimes I thought that this was the best thing ever, to be able to go where I liked, unseen and unheard, from the first-class Smoking Room to the tiny room that was home to Jim's family but other times it made me sad. For instance, here I was looking out over the railings of the Promenade Deck at the miles upon miles of blue water around me and I couldn't even remember what the sea smelled like.

Isobel would surely understand my situation if I could only talk to her. I felt her frustration when the shop-keepers got on *Titanic* at Queenstown, County Cork, to parade their wares before the passengers. Taking Sarah with her, Isobel told Jim that she just wanted to look at what was on sale. Naturally Jim didn't understand the point of *just* looking when she knew for certain that she couldn't afford to buy anything but, equally, he had been married long enough to know when to keep his mouth shut.

Meanwhile Joseph had his own worry. 'Do I have to go?' he asked.

His father laughed and suggested that they leave the women to it while they go and feed the seagulls some bread.

I followed Isobel and Sarah. Having spent the previous hour watching two men whack a small ball, with wooden racquets, against the wall of the squash court, in first class, I felt in need of more interesting company and I certainly found it in the crowd on deck. The traders, mostly women, spaced themselves out to set up shop with their goods, hoping to attract some of the wealthier passengers, in particular the Americans who were known to love all things Irish.

There was great excitement all round as the locals came out to see the biggest ship in the world. A brass band was playing on the Cork docks while over a hundred more passengers queued up to come onboard. An impressive mountain of mail and parcels, destined for America, waited to be loaded. Sarah's head twisted this way and that as she took in the hustle bustle, while her mother concentrated on being thrilled by the items for sale. Of course, the hard-nosed busi-nesswomen took little notice of her, guessing that they wer-en't going to make any money from her. Instead they lavished all their smiles and efforts on the better-dressed passengers who gathered around the lace, the cheeses, pots of jams and other knick-knacks, in sedate groups. I must admit, none of it appealed to me, but I could feel Isobel's huge longing to be able to buy something. First it was a fancy tablecloth, next it was some sort of lace blouse and then she hankered after a couple of yards of shiny material from which, she reasoned, she could make whatever she wanted.

She couldn't help herself; she was annoyed with her hus-band. *He might've offered a few pence. I wouldn't have taken it, but he could have offered it!*

Shifting Sarah onto her other hip, she watched enviously as two American women, in expensive hats and coats, attempted to haggle with the fierce little woman who was sell-ing the blouses. They ended up buying one each, with no dis-count, both thoroughly convinced that they had got the best deal for their dollars. Isobel smiled in spite of herself.

It was almost half past one. The new passengers had been checked in and the hundreds of postal bags stowed away on board. I spied *Titanic*'s captain watching the proceedings as the traders packed up and were sent on their way back to the mainland. Only then did Isobel realise for certain that she wouldn't be buying treats for either herself or the children. She surprised the both of us with her brief, silent outrage at the unfairness of her situation – too poor, as usual, for the price of the smallest item available. As much as she wanted a lace blouse, as much as she could clearly see it before her and clearly see herself wearing it, in her mind's eye, she just couldn't have it, no matter what. It was the same, I felt, about my wanting so badly to feel the wind on my face.

Titanic sounded her horn three times, in farewell to the Cork crowd who waved their handkerchiefs and parasols in reply. The brass band played on as the anchor was raised and *Titanic*'s mighty engine sounded out in earnest.

I remained on deck while Isobel and Sarah went in search of Jim and Joseph. Two stewards, who had been sweeping the deck clean, after all the visitors, stopped to watch the coast slowly recede into the distance. One of them waved just once to the onlookers, saying to his companion, 'Well, now. That's the last bit of land we'll see for a while.'

His friend shuddered, causing him to look up in surprise.

'What's wrong with you?'

The friend's face was a picture of confusion.

'I, I don't know. Just felt a chill, or something.'

'C'mon, let's get this done and we'll go get something to

eat. What we both need is one of Cookie's special pies and a nice, big mug of tea.'

I wished I could join them because I suddenly didn't feel right either. As I stared over the rails, into the ocean, I noticed the ship's reflection bubble up and down under the water, constantly changing in shape and colour. Nothing lasted forever or stayed the same. Where did I hear that before, in school or in church? That's why, I supposed, we had to keep moving forward and try our best not to look back. At least I think that was the solution.

Either way it was time once more, to leave Ireland behind and begin at last, the real journey, the real voyage, across the Atlantic Ocean to the New World of America.

Chapter Three

There was so much to do and see. I never had a dull moment, but that's not to say that I didn't find some things less exciting than others. For instance, I decided that I wouldn't bother watching any more squash; it wasn't nearly as interesting as watching football. Also, I got bored in the gym and the Turkish bathroom with its fussy towels and constant steam. I couldn't see the attraction of either of them and reckoned that perhaps having lots of money made you less imaginative about how to fill up your day. It was much more fun following the passengers around as they toured the decks, listening to their conversations.

I must admit, I had been impatient for the passengers to board the ship, to see if their reactions to her glorious interior matched how I felt about her. Even though I had watched everything being built from scratch, I still felt delighted all over again as I made my way through her different sections and compartments.

I was also struck by all the different work that went on throughout the day and the night. Down in the belly of the ship the fires that kept the engines going were kept burning by the stokers and greasers, who worked in shifts and were permanently covered in soot. There wasn't a lot to see, but it did remind me of working at the shipyard and hanging out with Charlie and the squad. Most of these men slept in small dormitories in third class, well away from the sensitivities of the richer passengers. I overheard two of them talking as they made their way back to their room, having shovelled coal for eight hours. They were filthy and their faces were shiny with a grimy sweat.

'So, you think we've the worse job on the ship?'

'Yep.'

'But we also have the most important?'

'She'd still be sitting on her backside in Belfast if it wasn't for us.'

'Hmm, that's a fair point.'

One of my favourite places was the third-class common room. It was nearly always full, crammed with all types of people who determined to enjoy themselves on such a beautiful ship. This was just the first part of their adventure. The real work began when they arrived in America and had to find themselves jobs and accommodation. A mixture of accents could be heard throughout: German, Italian, French and Swedish and, of course, English. In the evening, just like in first and second class, there was music provided by a few musicians who, unlike the band in first and second class, made a point of beckoning onstage anyone who cared to perform in whatever manner they could. Consequently, rowdy dancing and much singing was the norm after dinner, especially among the young single men and women.

There was plenty of children too as third class was mostly made up of people, like Jim and Isobel, who were emigrating to America, with their entire families, in search of a new life. Jim was rather like my mother, in that he didn't overtly push himself to get to know strangers, while Isobel reminded me of my father who had always considered strangers to be friends he hadn't made yet.

On the first afternoon, after we left Queenstown, while her husband refereed a slow, stumbling game of football for Joseph and some boys his age, Isobel shyly introduced herself to two girls who had joined the ship in Cork and had been giving the sleeping Sarah the fondest of smiles.

'She's beautiful. How old is she?' It was the older of the two, a friendly-looking girl with thick brown hair that matched the colour of her eyes.

A beaming Isobel replied proudly, 'Fourteen months

today. That's her brother over there, Joseph; he's six years old and the man doing his best to keep all the boys in line is my husband, Jim. I'm Isobel, by the way. And you two, if you don't mind me saying so, must be sisters. You're the image of one another.'

The girls laughed.

'Yes, I'm Maggie and this is my little sister Kate.'

Isobel was delighted. 'I was right! So, you're heading to America in search of fame and fortune ... or maybe a rich husband?'

The two sisters giggled and looked at one another, raising their eyebrows. A nod passed between them and Kate spoke, glancing around as if she was about to betray a promise of some sort, 'Well, the truth of it is, we sort of ran away from home.'

Isobel's eyes widened. 'Whatever do you mean?'

Maggie, the older girl, decided to take over. 'We're here with some neighbours from Longford. When they were buying their tickets, we asked them to get two for us in secret. Then we told them, at home, that we were only going to Queenstown, to see our friends off. Since we had to leave so early yesterday morning, nobody was up in time to see us bringing our bags with us. All we had to do, then, was board the ship.'

Isobel looked from one to the other. 'But won't your parents worry?'

'No. Well, not really. We're actually going over to family; we've two sisters and a brother already in America and we've been wanting to join them for ages.'

Kate butted in, wanting to supply all the important details, 'Our da died a few years ago and, after having thirteen kids, Mam is always sick, so our brother, who is the eldest, took charge of us all, but he's much too strict and won't let us go anywhere or do anything we fancy. He won't even let us go to the local dances in the town.'

Maggie nodded. 'We just want a chance to live a little. I'll write to Mam when we reach New York. She'll understand. I know she will. And there's plenty left at home for himself to boss around. We won't be missed.'

Isobel looked like she completely agreed with them. 'Well, I think you're both very brave and you're doing the right thing.' Then it was her turn to look secretive. She leant forward and lowered her voice, 'The thing is, Jim and I are also making an escape of sorts from our home.'

Naturally the girls were immediately intrigued, while Isobel checked that Jim was safely out of earshot. I also moved in closer, eager to hear what she had to say. As I hovered beside the sisters, Kate shivered slightly but was too focused on Isobel to question the sudden chill in the air around her.

With a slightly guilty look in the direction of her husband, who was still busily coaching the amateur footballers, Isobel felt that she had no choice now but to continue. Her listeners and I were waiting.

'We're both from Belfast, Jim and me. But from *different* parts.'

Here she sat back again, obviously expecting her listeners to understand what she was telling them. Instead the sisters waited politely, unsure of what they were supposed to say. Of course, I understood immediately but even I realised that for anyone who grew up elsewhere a bit more information was needed.

Isobel tried again. 'Jim is from west Belfast but I grew up in east Belfast.'

Riotous clapping started in a group a few tables away. A red-faced man stood up to sing some sort of ballad that involved lots of winking and face-pulling.

Still the two sisters looked blankly at one another, so that Isobel was obliged to throw Jim one last furtive look before blurting out as fast as she could, 'He's a Catholic and I'm a Protestant.'

'Oh, I see,' both sisters said simultaneously, causing the three of them to burst out laughing.

I, for one, was slightly shocked. I didn't think there were

any Catholics in my neighbourhood, not that I had anything against them particularly. I just never knew much about them nor do I remember them ever being mentioned by my mother or father. There were some Catholics working at the shipyard, but I always assumed that they were nowhere near me.

My uncle told me that they were usually *very* good at whatever trade they specialised in. 'They have to be or they'd be sent packing long before lunch.'

He also told me that they sometimes got a rough time from the others: 'Ach, sure it's bound to happen. Gangs of neighbours who have known each other for years, going to the same schools, churches, pubs and then along comes a stranger, from a different part of town, with whom they have little or nothing in common.'

When I asked Al why, he shrugged. 'They're just "different", that's all. We're proud to be part of the British Empire, while they prefer to follow the old pope in Rome. Doesn't make sense, really. One thing is for sure, though, you can always spot them coming. There's just something about them.'

I certainly hadn't suspected anything different about Jim; he looked no different from any other man I had ever met. Then again, maybe I was a bit soft about this sort of thing.

Neither Ed nor Charlie had been friendly to Jim when he approached him that rainy afternoon. Could it be that they recognised he was one of 'them'?

'Was there much trouble for you?' asked Maggie.

'Not really, but we did our best not to draw any attention to ourselves. We lived in east Belfast. You never know how people will react, so it made more sense to pretend we were like everyone else on the street. Joseph was sent to the local school and Jim came with us to church on Sunday. He felt we had to be seen to fit in, for our peace of mind.'

Kate looked over at Jim – who was blissfully ignorant of the attention he was receiving – unable to stop herself from saying, 'Oooh, how romantic!'

Isobel giggled, shaking her head. 'I wouldn't call it that, but I think I know what you mean.'

Maggie hadn't finished with her questions, 'What about your families, they must have known?'

Here Isobel took a second to remove an invisible loose thread from the cuff of her sleeve. Maggie became embarrassed as she immediately understood that the subject was no longer a laughing matter. 'Oh dear, I'm so sorry. I'm too nosey for my own good.'

Her younger sister nodded in vibrant agreement. However, Isobel rushed to put the blushing girls at ease again. 'Ah, don't mind me. Besides I didn't have to tell you anything. It is sad, though. Nobody turned up at our wedding, after much abuse, from *both* sides, I might add. Plus it was made clear that we were no longer welcome in our own parents' homes ... even now, seven years later.'

She glanced at the girls in turn, her voice cracking slightly, and murmured, 'I mean, they've never even met the children.'

Wanting to move things back on to a more positive footing, Maggie quickly offered, 'So you decided to make a new life for yourselves, far away from angry relatives?'

Doing her best to blink away her tears, Isobel forced out a genuine smile, and agreed, 'Yes, that's it. Just like yourselves.'

The red-faced man was still singing away, in the corner. The bawdy ballad finished, he had moved on to something more serious or sad, or both. To demonstrate his change of mood, he held out his hands in front of him, like he was begging for mercy, and closed his eyes as he struggled courageously, but in vain, over the higher notes. Therefore, he had no idea that he was the butt of many jokes throughout the room.

'His relatives are probably having a party in Ireland, now that they've got rid of him,' whispered Maggie.

'Just a pity we've to listen to him now!' added her sister.

Tears streamed down Isobel's face, but this time, much to Maggie and Kate's relief, they were of laughter.

Chapter Four

That evening I decided, for a change, to 'have dinner' with the toffs in the first-class dining room. As soon as the bugle sounded out at 7pm, calling the diners to dine, I rushed to join them. The whole first-class experience fascinated me. For one thing these people with their top hats and sparkling jewels had paid a whopping £870 each for their first-class ticket. This meant, however, that they could use any of the facilities for free: the gym, the squash court, the swimming pool, the Turkish bath and all the food they could possibly eat. I had never known such wealth existed. Of course their section of *Titanic*, far away from the lower-class passengers, held the most incredible sights of the entire ship. Even the light switches, in the corridors and rooms, were very fanciful, compared to the switches in second or third class. They were made to look like porcelain ornaments on the walls.

Each first-class compartment had its very own luxury

bathroom. In third class there were just two baths for hun-dreds of steerage passengers. This meant either getting up very early or else being prepared to stand in a long queue of men and women, hoping that whatever bath you finally got to use wasn't too dirty from the hundreds ahead of you. Although I had noticed that, so far, the Europeans were the only ones who were interested in washing themselves every day. At home I used to have, like Ma and Da, my weekly bath on a Saturday night. That afternoon, in the common room, Isobel had told the girls where the baths could be found. The sisters thanked her but assured her they probably wouldn't need to take one since they had had a good wash the night before they came onboard.

'Yes,' said Maggie. 'Sure I can wait 'til we get to our sister's place in New York.'

The first-class dining room was the most beautiful place I had ever seen. Since I have never been in one, I wondered if this was what a hotel looked like. The best hotel in Belfast was probably Central Hotel, but I'm sure that even this was no match for this dining room. It stretched the full width of *Titanic*, which meant it was 114 feet long, and it was big enough to have over 500 people eating their dinner at the exact same time.

During the day there were long tables covered by all

different kinds of food, so that the wealthy passengers did not go hungry between meals. Smelly stuff like shrimp, salmon mayonnaise and smoked herrings. For those who didn't like fish there was plenty of meat like veal, roast beef and ham pies. Not that I knew straight away what I was looking at and I only learned that the fish stuff was smelly because the two boys, whose job it was to wash and peel the thousands of potatoes, had crinkled up their noses and asked one of the junior cooks if the pink things were worms. The cook looked at them as if they were the most stupid people he had ever met, exclaiming, 'Worms! Are you having me on? This here is shrimp ... fish ... as in from the sea. You do know what fish is, don't you?' The boys were quick to say yes. A few seconds later the cook, who obviously relished his new role as a teacher – though not a very nice one – whirled by with another dish, asking loudly, 'And would I be right in think-ing you wouldn't know what this is either?' The boys, who were much too timid, glanced at one another before confirm-ing with blushing looks that the snotty man was exactly right. He gloated, pleased with his little victory, 'Huh! Thought as much. Well, I'll tell you what it is then. This here, my lads, is veal, that is, the offspring of a cow.' One of the boys, the tall-est one who was maybe sixteen or so, nodded a little too quickly, raising suspicions immediately. The cook snapped at him eagerly, 'So, clever clogs, tell us what it is then.' I wanted to cheer when the lad nervously stuttered out, much to the cook's disappointment, the correct answer: 'C-calf?'

A lot of this food went to waste daily because it would be hard, I suppose, to eat in between such enormous meals as this:

Luncheon Menu

Consommé fermier   Cock-a-leekie soup
Fillets of Brill
Chicken à la Maryland
Corned Beef, Vegetables, Dumplings

From the Grill
Grilled Mutton Chops
Mashed, Fried & Baked Jacket Potatoes

Custard Pudding
Apple Meringue   Pastry

And there was even more to the menu than that. A whole lot of things from the buffet and *eight* different cheeses. Apart from the potatoes, I don't think I've ever tasted anything else.

Captain Smith ate in the first-class dining room every evening and there was always a polite scrum to sit at his table. He was exactly how I pictured a ship's captain to be: medium height, old, white hair, neat white beard and his prestigious uniform smart enough to hide his lumpish figure.

Known as the 'Millionaires' Captain', he was a great favourite with the toffs. They treated him like he was some sort of royalty. Then again, when I thought about it, a ship in the middle of the ocean, miles away from any country, is a bit like an island in itself. The passengers are like the island's population, with rich and poor living in different parts of the same place – just like any town. So, there has to be someone in charge, someone whose responsibility is to tell everyone else what to do. On *Titanic*, this position was held by Captain Edward Smith. There was no one higher than him on board. Therefore, he was exactly like a king or a president and that is why the richest and best passengers wanted to sit at his dinner table. It was a great privilege and meant that they were important too.

I joined his group that night, but as nobody knew I was there I didn't feel any more important than usual. Everyone in the room was dressed up as if they were going to a ball. The men wore impeccable suits and shoes that looked like they had never touched the ground. Meanwhile the women outdid one another in long, sleeveless evening gowns and chains of jewels that glistened about their throats and wrists. Even the stewards, waitresses and the musicians looked better dressed than the ones in second and third class.

Conversation was already in full flow at the captain's table.

'But, my dear, I thought you liked the pyramids. I'm certain you said you did when we were there in front of them.'

'Well, yes, they were very grand when we first saw them but then, after a few minutes, I found myself wondering ho hum, is that it? I'm sure you'll agree with me, Captain Smith, that they are rather plain and just a bit ... well ... boring, when all is said and done.'

The captain took a moment to consider his feelings about one of the great wonders of the world.

'I dare say, Lady Duff Gordon, that the Egyptian pyramids probably appeal more to men, especially engineers and historians. They are certainly plain when compared to the exquisite paintings and sculptures that can be found in the great galleries of Europe. And, of course, any lady of refined tastes would prefer to gaze upon something a bit more complex or, indeed, delicate.'

The plump, overdressed woman sitting two chairs away from the captain wasn't like the others at the table. She was quite outspoken and given to making lots of jokes, regardless of the sometimes chilly atmosphere that greeted her appearance in the first-class dining room and lounge. Mrs Brown was American and I had discovered the peculiar reason that some of the other toffs didn't much like her; she was '*nouveau riche*' (French for 'the new rich'). This meant that she had only been rich for a short time, and so hadn't been born into a wealthy family like most of the other first-class passengers. Her husband became a millionaire overnight, about twenty years earlier, when the mine he worked at struck gold – and lots of it.

Turning now to Captain Smith, with a mischievous smile on her face, she asked, 'Or do you mean, Captain, something like *Titanic*? Do you consider her to be complex and delicate?'

The captain laughed a little. 'Well, now, Mrs Brown, I suppose that depends on who is gazing upon her. It has taken many men many, many months to design and build this ship, so you might say that yes, she is most definitely complex. On the other hand, she is, you will be glad to hear, as far from delicate as one would wish.'

Lady Duff Gordon's husband spoke up once more, 'She's unsinkable, isn't she, or practically, at any rate? That's how Harland & Wolff describe her, "practically unsinkable" – which amounts to the same thing in my mind.'

Captain Smith picked up his wine glass and gently swirled the contents before putting it back on the table. 'At 882 feet long and weighing over 46,000 tones, *Titanic* represents a dynamic leap not just in the shipbuilding industry but for all of us. Perhaps it is not enough to say that she is the biggest in the world – perhaps one could go further and describe her as the most modern, most perfect machine that has ever been created.'

One of the other women looked around their table before saying, 'Well, I certainly couldn't imagine anything bigger or better than her. Is Lord Duff Gordon correct then, Captain? She is unsinkable?'

'As her captain I can only say, with hand on heart, that I can see no reason for this ship to flounder.'

'Aha!' said Lord Duff Gordon, holding up his glass to his fellow diners. 'That's more than good enough for me.'

They all laughed while Lady Duff Gordon called out, 'Oh, I say, here's Mr Andrews.'

I liked Mr Andrews. He was the engineer who had helped design *Titanic* and I knew from Uncle Al that he was a real favourite in the offices of Harland & Wolff. From what I could gather his greatest trait was that he treated all men equally, from his fellow engineers to the gawkiest catch-boy. Certainly I had followed him as he strolled through the ship, on his daily rounds, and watched him greet housekeeping staff in much the same way as he greeted first-class passengers. I even remember Ed speaking fondly about him – an unusual occurrence for the sarcastic riveter. 'That Mr Andrews treats a man as a man, no matter who he is or how little money he has.'

Mr Andrews approached the captain's table, smiling shyly under the warm gaze of all the excited ladies.

'Good evening, everyone. I hope you are enjoying your dinner.'

Mrs Brown spoke first, commanding his attention, before anyone else could thwart her, 'Well, I think it would go down a lot sweeter if you were to join us.'

Every other man at the table looked suitably insulted at this while the gentle ladies fought the urge to roll their eyes at one another. I could hear exactly what Lady Duff Gordon was thinking, and, not surprisingly, it wasn't at all complimentary: *Awful woman, with her ridiculous pronunciation and dreadful taste in clothes. Why must she sit at our table? It's not right. She has the manners of a chimney sweep.*

Meanwhile, Captain Smith continued to cut and fork his food in a subtle show of studied indifference.

Mr Andrews actually blushed but was determined not to let the loud but well-meaning woman feel any embarrassment on his account. 'Mrs Brown, it would be churlish of me to refuse such a flattering invitation. However, I shall just have coffee as I've already eaten.'

'That's absolutely fine, or "grand", as my pa would say. He's Irish, you know. We were just talking now about your lovely ship. You must be so very proud of her.'

With a speedy glance sideways at the captain's blank expression, Mr Andrews proceeded carefully, wanting to shed himself of the limelight, without causing any offence. Unlike Captain Smith, he didn't crave the company of the grandest passengers and more often than not just ate something simple in his cabin as he worked on his drawings and measurements. I overheard him telling Charles Joughin, one of the head bakers, that as much as he was enjoying sailing – at last – on *Titanic*, he hated being away from his wife and baby daughter. The baker, an extremely friendly and kind-hearted man, went away with a thoughtful look on his face only to reappear a short while later with a specially baked loaf for the engineer, promising that there would be plenty more.

'Oh, it's not just me. We are all delighted with her,

though, of course, she's not perfect yet but I'm working on that.'

Polite silence and puzzled smiles greeted him and he felt obliged to give more details. 'I suppose there's always room for improvement with just about anything you could think of and *Titanic* is certainly no different. For instance, how many of you ladies have found much use for the rather ample Reading and Writing Room?'

I knew what he was going to say. The Ladies' Reading and Writing Room had been built just for the women of first class; only they hardly ever went near it.

Mrs Brown looked around her companions and found that they were in grudging agreement with her which made her giddy inside. *Hah! Silly prudes with their turned-up noses and yellow teeth. Well, it seems, my ladies, that we're not so different after all.* 'It is a most pretty space, with its white walls and elegant furniture, but, to be perfectly honest, its immense size makes me feel almost lonely as any other occupants always seem so far away from wherever I choose to sit.'

'That is exactly right, Mrs Brown,' agreed Mr Andrews, 'I'm afraid it's a bit of a blunder on my part. I had thought that each evening, upon finishing dinner, the ladies would leave the men to their cigars and brandy and retire to the Reading and Writing Room, which only goes to show how out of step I am in these modern times.'

'Oh, but you're not, Mr Andrews,' said Lady Duff Gordon. 'I can assure you that at home I would, after dinner, lead my female guests to the sitting room, leaving the men to talk business in peace, but because there's an orchestra here, and coffee is served up to us, I prefer to remain where I am.'

'I completely understand, my lady, and this is why I'm making plans about reducing the Reading and Writing Room to half its size, thus allowing for the construction of two new rooms.'

One of the other gentlemen had the look of someone who knows they are about to say something of the utmost importance. 'I presume, sir, that this is the point of your own voyage, to fix problems as they crop up. For instance you must observe how things go at sea as the final test of your design, as it were.'

'Indeed, but, of course, every ship that is first sent out by Harland & Wolff is accompanied by a Guarantee Group for exactly that purpose. In this way if anything goes wrong, then the experts, the ones who have built her, are on site to fix or even just advise.'

'Excellent!' exclaimed Mrs Brown. 'So we are in good hands?'

'The very best, Mrs Brown. I have brought with me some

of Belfast's finest apprentice engineers, plumbers and electricians. Two or three of them are still quite young but they have been selected because they are top in their field. Harland & Wolff prides itself on nurturing those who show promise.'

My uncle Al had told me all about this. It was a huge honour to be asked to go along on a ship's maiden voyage because it meant that your work was rated highly by the company and therefore your job was secure.

Mr Andrews had brought eight men and boys with him. I had come to know them over the last two days.

First was his good friend Scotsman Roderick Chisholm. Mr Chisholm was Chief Draughtsman and had designed *Titanic*'s lifeboats, and was under strict orders from his wife and children to bring them back something nice from New York.

Anthony Frost was Chief Fitter and he was the only one out of the group to have spent any time at sea. His wife, Lizzie, and his four children were impatiently awaiting his return, so that they could hear all about life onboard the glamorous ship. Anthony had helped to choose young Alfred Cunningham, apprentice fitter, to be his assistant. Alfred couldn't believe his luck and promised his excited brothers and sisters that he would remember every single thing about his experience, so that he could tell them all about it.

The ship's electrics were under the watch of William Parr. From Monday to Saturday Mr Parr was Assistant Manager in Harland & Wolff's electrical department. On Sundays, however, his only day off, he taught scripture to children at his local church. He also had an apprentice, eighteen-year-old Ennis Hastings Watson. Still living at home with his parents, Ennis had studied his trade at the Belfast Municipal Technical Institute. A serious boy, he had little time for a social life, yet he found himself striking up a friendship with two younger members of the group, Francis and William. Apprentice plumber Francis Parks lived in Belfast with his parents, three brothers and two sisters. In fact his three older brothers also worked at Harland & Wolff, yet it was he who was chosen for *Titanic*'s maiden voyage, a fact he broadcasted several times over, at the dinner table, until his mother told him to stop showing off, laughing as she did so. Apprentice joiner William Campbell's parents were good friends with the Parks and William, the youngest of the group, treated Francis as the big brother he'd never had.

There was quite a difference between a pristine ship sitting in its dry dock and a pristine ship being let loose on the ocean. For an electrician, plumber or carpenter to appreciate how their piece of effort contributed to the entire jigsaw of the ship, as a whole, they simply had to be there with her as she rode the waves and pushed through the stormy gales or glided easily in the good weather. It was a fine reward for an employee, no matter how little they were actually needed.

I had stood beside Mr Andrews as he had welcomed his team onboard:

'You mightn't have a whole lot to do, boys, but I want you all to observe closely how the ship reacts on the water, and, it goes without saying, make yourselves known to the crew. Teach them as much as they need to know. But don't forget to enjoy yourselves too.'

I felt Mr Andrews' impatience to leave the dining room. His coffee cup was empty and he longed for the solitude of his private quarters. He also guessed that the captain disliked sharing his guests' attention with him and was eager for him to be gone. Therefore, as soon as he judged it safe enough to excuse himself, he slowly rose to his feet, explaining that unfortunately he had to go back to work.

Watching him leave, I considered what to do next. With the departure of the engineer the conversation at the captain's table grew quite formal again and I was soon bored. Moving in and around the hundreds of rectangular tables, I was filled once more, despite my mood, with awe for the magnificence of this luxurious and vast hall. Surely it was a match for the

King's palace in London: the fancy tiles on the sea-blue floor, with their red and gold pattern, the panelled ceiling, the heavy, white linen tablecloths and the sparkling crystal. Each table was lit by its own electrical lamp, the rose-coloured shades making a fine contrast against the spotless tablecloths. The guests were exquisite in their finery, even the plain old men sporting double chins and their unsmiling podgy wives who merely frowned their thanks at the efficiency of their waiters. There was no raucous laughter or rude ballads; instead the band played soothing and genteel music. I fancied that only the most proper of words were used and the most proper of events took place here, with no surprises and nothing to worry about. So, what was it exactly that I liked about being here? I might have expected to feel suffocated or even intimidated but really I just felt safe.

I knew what I planned to do the following night; I was attending a birthday party for Oscar, one of the Post Office workers, and was very much looking forward to it. The postal team was made up of three Americans and two Englishmen and they seemed to be the best of friends. They worked up quite a sweat in the Mail Room, with their shirtsleeves permanently rolled up to the elbow, constantly teasing one another as they quickly sorted through the millions of letters that were addressed to houses all over America and Canada.

Their 'office' was on the lower deck, alongside some third-class cabins and cabins occupied by the hard-working stokers and greasers. Since they were so far away from the 'fancy' passengers they were free to indulge themselves in practical jokes and great gales of laughter that usually involved at least one of them doubled over trying to catch his breath. I was delighted to be there when the Englishmen decided to get the Americans back for some trick earlier. One of them got into one of the huge postbags, which were almost as tall as themselves, while the second man tied the neck loosely, allowing air to get in. Then, when the three Americans arrived, two of them went to open the nearest bag to their bench and actually screamed like little girls when the English bloke jumped out and roared, 'BOOOO!' at the top of his voice. We all laughed for a good ten minutes over that. Anyway I was saving them for the next night.

For the rest of the evening I would keep company with the two Marconi-operators, Jack Phillips and his young assistant Harold Bride.

Chapter Five

The Marconi-office was quite small and the alcove of the office, where the two operators took turns to sleep, was absolutely tiny. They lived on the Boat Deck, which was quite a busy one. Apart from the Marconi-room there was the Post Office, separate from its sister Mail Room below, and the second-class Library Room. There was also a lot of crew living on this deck, to the front of the ship, along with first-class staterooms, dayrooms and suites.

When I called in earlier, the two young men were yawning and rubbing their eyes, tired from working at a frantic pace for too many hours. Like the postal workers, they were responsible for communication, although theirs was of a more immediate kind. They spent all day tapping out messages from and for *Titanic*'s passengers. The passengers wrote out their notes by hand, using as few words as possible, at the purser's inquiry desk, paying twelve shillings and six pence for the first ten words and then nine pence for each word after that. Since it wasn't cheap, it was mostly the first-class passengers who made use of the service. The purser counted up the words, took their money, rolled up the telegram and placed it in a tube that ran all the way to the wall of the Marconi-room. Here the messages popped out and all Jack or Harold had to do was read them, make note of the amount of words per telegram and then tap them out, across the ocean: *dit, dit, dit, dah, dah, dah*. It was hard to believe that those little bleeps meant actual words to someone who was seated at a desk just like this but miles and miles away from *Titanic*.

Most of their business seemed to involve such luminous pieces of information as:

HELLO FROM TITANIC. PLAYING LOTS OF SQUASH IN ANTICIPATION OF OUR NEXT TENNIS MATCH.

and

HOPE YOU ARE ENJOYING YOUR TRIP. HOW ABOUT LUNCHEON ON THE 23RD?

Despite the fact they worked in shifts, the hours they spent at their desk seemed to be more than the hours they spent away from it. Since leaving Southampton, over thirty hours ago, they had sent and received over 250 telegrams. Then, on top of an already heavy workload, they had a faulty machine to deal with. Only the previous day, while I was visiting, the Marconi-transmitter ceased to work electronically which meant that it was relying solely on its battery. This wasn't much use to *Titanic* in the middle of the Atlantic Ocean. A battery-operated transmitter could only send and receive messages within a radius of eighty miles while the electrics increased that range to a vastly superior 250 miles.

When I checked on them, that morning, the messages were mounting up and going nowhere. Jack opened up the *Marconi Rule Book*, in the hope of discovering some helpful information. He sighed loudly, a few minutes later, as he slammed it shut again.

Harold shrugged. 'I told you. We'll have to wait to have it fixed by an actual Marconi-engineer. Although I do think there should be a Plan B if the machine happens to be miles and miles away from such a person.'

Too annoyed to make a reply to this, Jack merely scowled at the fresh bundle of notes that were waiting to be sent out across the ocean. Those notes meant lots of unhappy customers and, therefore, a loss of precious earnings. He eyed his partner who was busy tapping away in receipt of yet another ice warning.

'You know, we could try fixing it ourselves. I reckon that, between us, we could do it.'

Harold grinned as he picked up the next message, an impossible one to send on the battery.

'Yep. Like I said, it does seem silly to have to wait until we get to America. It's not like Head Office can see the amount of messages that are waiting to go.'

'Okay, then. We'll do it tonight, when it's quiet.'

Later that night, by the time I arrived they were bent over the transmitter, already surrounded by wires, nuts and bolts. Jack was manning the operation like a doctor while Harold played nurse, patiently holding various pieces of machinery and making little suggestions only when he felt it necessary. Intrigued, I moved in to get a close-up of what they were doing. Harold shivered suddenly and looked about himself in obvious puzzlement.

'What's up with you?' asked Jack.

'I don't know. I keep thinking that someone is standing over me.'

Jack rolled his eyes. 'You and your guilty conscience. You're just worried that old Mr Marconi is suddenly going to

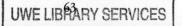

appear and catch us taking his transmitter apart with our grubby, little hands.'

Harold grinned and said, 'Laugh away, but just remember this was all your idea.'

Jack glanced up at the clock on the wall. 'Oh dear, I've a feeling this is going to take a lot longer than I thought.'

'Don't worry about it. Really, I don't mind. I remember spending all night working on this antenna I set up in my parents' back garden. The neighbours didn't know what to make of it.'

'Fair enough, then.' Nodding his head towards the thick bundle of unsent messages, Jack gave a mild sigh, 'It's going to be a very busy day for us tomorrow.'

⚜ ⚜ ⚜

I decided to leave the telegraphists to it, watching them fix the transmitter wasn't very interesting, so I headed back out into the ship to see what else was happening. As soon as I spotted the bandleader from the first-class dining room, I followed him to see where he was going. He reached into his pockets for his cigarettes, his violin case knocking against his hip as he walked out the door onto the deck outside, obviously wanting a breath of fresh air. If he was looking for peace and quiet, he would have been disappointed as he was accosted as soon as he stepped outside.

'Hello there. Mr Hartley, isn't it, from the orchestra? I'm Charles Joughin, Chief Baker.'

The two men shook hands. 'Please, call me Wallace. Gosh, I didn't expect it to be so busy out here.'

The bandleader put a cigarette in his mouth, prompting the baker to step forward and light it for him. 'Yes, it's one of the reasons that I like coming out here myself. There's always a great mixture on this deck: second- and third-class passengers wanting a break from the crowd inside and then the likes of those young bellboys over there, who are, no doubt, hiding from their supervisor – oh, they're gone! I didn't see them leave.'

Both Wallace and I stared politely at the empty space, while Charles scratched his head before continuing on, 'They're far too young to be smoking anyway. Cheeky monkeys!'

Having no opinion on the subject, the musician blew a thin line of smoke into the sky. Charles, glancing around quickly, took out a small bottle from his inside pocket and raised it in invitation.

'No thank you, Charles, I never drink when I'm working.'

The baker nodded in agreement. 'Right you are. I'm just taking a sip because it's a cold night, though I hear it's about to get even colder. So, tell me, how are you enjoying your trip?'

The musician laughed as he leant against the railings. 'Oh very well, indeed. And yourself?'

'I'd be lying if I said I wasn't. The truth of it is, Wallace, I enjoy my job. It's hard going, mind you, working long hours to feed such big numbers. Yet, I must say, I wouldn't have it any other way. I mean, I've worked on plenty of other ships, but I've never had so much to do before. I'm in charge of all the bread, all the baking, and I also run the second-class kitchen. Of course, the pay is better too, so I really can't complain.'

The two men puffed away in comfortable silence for a few seconds, until the baker added, 'To be honest, it's a bit of a privilege to be on the biggest ship in the world. Would you agree?'

Wallace, who had started to hum softly, smiled in appreciation and agreed, 'It is a very magnificent ship all right, by far the nicest one I've ever been on. Most of the musicians have played on other ships too, but we're all delighted to be onboard *Titanic*. There's something about her that feels different from the others. A couple of us have even remarked that our instruments sound sweeter in the luxurious surroundings – but that probably sounds silly.'

The baker gave his companion a thoughtful look and found himself saying, 'No, I think I understand what you mean. I don't know about you but I got a chance to tour her before any of the passengers came aboard and, well, every now and then, I could have sworn I heard footsteps. I would turn to see who was behind me to find that I was completely alone.'

Wallace looked surprised at the turn the conversation had taken. 'You mean you think the ship is ... haunted?'

'Maybe. Well, why not? I'm sure plenty died in the making of her. Or maybe it's the spirit of *Titanic* herself. Doesn't it seem to you that she could be a breathing, living thing, with all this light, heat and electricity pumping through her veins?'

For an answer Wallace turned to look the ship over, from where they stood. His fingers tapped out a tune against the case, keeping an unconscious rhythm, I felt, with the chug-chugging – the mechanical heart-beat – of *Titanic*'s engines.

For my part I loved to think that *Titanic* was alive and committed to her role of looking after her passengers and crew, ferrying them safely across the world, keeping them warm and dry, no matter what the weather was like. Also, the baker wasn't mistaken in thinking he was being followed that day. I hadn't bargained on him being that sensitive. His calling out, 'Hello, who's there?' gave me no end of fun. However, I had a bit of a fright when I continued to hear footsteps after we had stopped moving, along with what sounded like the faint rustle of a dress.

'How many pieces of music do you play each day? You don't just do the same things over and over again, do you?'

Wallace shuddered. 'Lord, no. Well, unless a passenger requests his favourite tune on a daily basis. We have the entire *White Star Line Song Book* as our repertoire; every musician has to know the 352 songs off by heart.'

Charles whistled in wonder and asked, 'Tell me, now, how on earth do you manage to remember them all?'

Patting the violin case, Wallace laughed and shrugged at the same time. 'Whatever I forget, she always remembers.'

Charles gave the case a respectful nod. I had a feeling that this was the nearest he had ever been to an instrument before. He flashed the musician a look of new appreciation. 'You and me have something in common. What I mean is, we're both lucky enough to be paid for doing something we love to do. For instance, would I be right in thinking that you'd make music for free, if you could afford to, because that's the way I feel about creating new recipes for bread and pastries?' Wallace answered him, nodding enthusiastically, 'Yes, you're absolutely right, and it's something that I would never take for granted. I have friends who spend sixty hours a week standing on a factory floor, repeating the same little job over and over again and, while I admire them for their fortitude, I know full well that sort of life isn't for me. It would be like locking me into a cage.'

He took another drag on his cigarette and threw the baker a sidelong glance before continuing on, 'Perhaps I'm daft but I like to think that there's a plan for all of us and only a few of us are lucky to discover it at all. Most of us don't realise that we could be looking for something more than what our neighbours are doing. Sometimes I wonder how my life would have turned out had my grandfather not left this violin to my father, who had no interest in music yet always encouraged me from that first moment I placed her under my chin.'

'Me too,' said Charles, 'my dear old nan had me kneading dough when I was three years of age. Imagine that! She said it was on account of there being no money to buy me toys, plus she needed the help too.'

Wallace glanced quickly at the baker, to see if he was pulling his leg and realised, from his earnest expression, that he was completely serious.

Charles flicked the butt of his cigarette into the sea and took out his pocket watch to check the time. 'Whoops, I'd better head off in a minute. You never finished telling me about the sort of music you play.'

Sending his butt into the water after Charles', Wallace replied, 'Ordinarily, we cover a wide choice, from operatic pieces to classical music. You know, Tchaikovsky, Schubert, Verdi, nothing too heavy, mind. And then we also play the latest dancehall hits.'

Charles grinned. 'Ah, but could you do one of my favourite songs at the minute?'

With that he began to sing softly, well aware that he really couldn't sing very well at all:

♩ ♪ ♩ ♪ ♪ *'Oh I do like to be beside the seaside;*

I do like to be beside the sea' ♩ ♪ ♩ ♪ ♪

Wallace did his best not to laugh at the blushing baker. Clamping his hand over his mouth so that his smile could hardly be seen, he was delighted to report that he and his band could perform that song very well indeed.

⚜ ⚜ ⚜

'Well done,' declared Harold in the Marconi-room. 'What a relief to be back at full strength. Look, why don't you head off to bed? I'll clean up here and then I want to finish today's paperwork. We'll just take turns, tomorrow, to get through the back-log.'

Jack's look was one of gratitude. 'Are you sure? That would be great. I really need to get my head down for a few hours. I hardly know what day it is, I'm that tired.'

Harold winked at him as he pulled out the accounts ledger, 'It's just after 2 o'clock on Sunday morning, on the 14th of April in the year 1912.'

'Ha, Ha! Very funny!'

❖ ❖ ❖

Jack must have fallen asleep the minute his head hit the pillow because he began snoring almost immediately. Harold smiled to himself. He was counting up the words in the telegrams in front of them, making sure they balanced with the amount calculated against the total charged by the purser. The room's atmosphere was soothing, thanks to the ticking clock and the distant rumbling of the engines.

Of course Harold wasn't the only person to be working at this hour. Plates, cups and cutlery were being washed, dried and stacked throughout the three kitchens, by sleepy boys, in time for the bakers who had to be up well before dawn to make the dough for the bread for the thousands of breakfasts that had to be served up in the morning. Glasses were still being polished clean in the first-class lounge; the late-night card players were always the last to retire to bed. Down below, the engines were being kept going by the night shift of stokers, greasers and engineers. In the bridge a sailor was at the wheel, keeping the ship on course, under the watchful eye of the commanding officer. While above us all there were two lookouts in the crow's nest, keeping an eye out for obstacles ahead.

As for the passengers, mothers were changing nappies and feeding bottles to the tiny babies who had yet to recognise the difference between night and day. Fathers comforted their children who had woken up in confusion, telling them that whatever it was, it was only a bad dream.

All was exactly as it should be.

'Ugh, what? What do you want?' Jack's tone was sharp, making Harold jump a little.

'What *are* you talking about?' he called through to Jack in the adjoining room.

'What do you mean, what am *I* talking about?'

Harold stared at the ceiling above him, muttering under his breath, 'For heaven's sake.' Then, he raised his voice again, 'Jack, what's the matter?'

'I don't know. You called me. Has the machine broken again?'

Rubbing his hand through his hair, Harold sighed, 'No,

the machine is not broken and no, I was not calling for you.'

'Yes, you were. You woke me up, didn't you?'

'Nope,' was the short reply.

'Whoops, sorry! I must have been dreaming.'

But it wasn't a dream, or – at least – it couldn't have been, because I heard something too and I wouldn't have thought it was possible for anyone else to share my dreams. It sounded like frantic whispering, blurred, hushed words that I couldn't make out. And yes I was sure that in the midst of these strange voices, I recognised Jack's, calling out for his friend. What on earth did it mean?

In the silence that followed, the ticking of the clock was allowed to dominate once more.

Chapter Six

I decided to spend some time with Jim and his family, hoping that I'd shake off this strangeness that was beginning to scare me a little. They were in the dining room, trying to talk to one another over the noise of their fellow diners. Joseph had to shout to get his sister's attention. She was sitting on her father's lap, eyeing up his roast beef and boiled potatoes that were sitting in puddles of gravy. 'SARAH? Sarah, can you do this?' He was trying to teach her how to clap her hands, but the lesson wasn't proving very successful. She stared at him politely, for maybe two seconds, before returning to her father's fork which climbed past her face with amazing regularity.

Isobel laughed. 'Oh dear, she's not a very good student, is she Joe?'

Joseph shrugged politely, not wanting to say what he really felt, knowing it might get him into trouble: *She's stupid and boring, and they knew I wanted a brother. I told them I only wanted brothers. It's not fair!*

74

After tea I made my way to the little room that the postal workers shared. I wasn't having a good day and hoped that the birthday party would take my mind off the tension that was gnawing at me, although I did laugh when I discovered young Joseph stealing the cutlery and hiding it in the family's tattered suitcase. He planned to surprise his mother with it in their new home in America. Isobel had marvelled over the variety of spoons, forks, and knives, all decorated with the White Star Line logo and now, unknown to her, she would have some of her very own forevermore.

I could hear the cheering all the way down the corridor. 'Congratulations Oscar, on arriving at yet another birthday.'

The American with the red curly hair and round spectacles led the applause for the birthday boy whose face was red with a mixture of happiness and embarrassment. One of the Englishmen called for the cake to be cut. It wasn't a very big one, enough for a slice each for the five men, but it did look nice with its yellow sponge, red jam and scoops of cream. There were five tiny candles standing up in it; the pin-sized flames threw shadows across the walls of the dormitory.

'Yes, come on, William. Get a move on, the cream is melting.'

The American pretended to be shocked. 'Oh my goodness. Don't you British know anything? Oscar, ignore them.

Make a speech, followed by a secret wish, then blow out your candles, and *then* cut the cake.'

Oscar winked at the others. 'I'll tell you all now what my wish is. I wish that William would give me his spectacles, so that I can use them to find the ridiculously small candles on my small cake. How's that then?'

William wagged his finger in his friend's face. 'Now, Oscar, you're one of my best chums, so you know that I wouldn't take my glasses off for anyone, not even you.'

The other American, John, turned to the two Englishmen and said, 'He's not joking either. He even wears them in bed, in case he loses them.'

There was more laughter and lots more joking around, but I had stopped listening. Instead I was staring at the wall behind William and Oscar who were bent over the cake. Five postal workers and me – only, one thing that I lost in my fatal accident was a shadow. Five postal workers should have meant five shadows. So, why was it that I could make out almost double that? No, no, that couldn't be right.

I left the room in a hurry, suddenly aware of how lonely I was. I don't know if I was exactly scared. I mean, what had I to be scared off in my state? Surely nothing more could touch me. Nevertheless, for perhaps the first time in almost two years, I longed to be back in Belfast, with my mother and father. I wanted to go back home, go back in time to when I was just a child who knew nothing at all about anything much.

'It's a peculiar night, isn't it? Perfectly still and quiet. All those stars and no sign of the moon.' It was a woman's voice. There were still a few passengers on deck, taking a last stroll of the evening. One couple was standing at the railing, peering out into the darkness. The wife pulled her coat more tightly around her. It was obviously very cold because I could see the air they exhaled upon speaking. The husband was finishing his cigar and mused, 'I wonder what the temperature is. It must be near freezing. I think I can make out icebergs. Look over there; can you see what I mean?'

The woman strained her eyes to see, before replying, 'Yes, I can just about make out something there. They look like boulders in the water.'

'Well, yes. Those small ones are called growlers, I believe.'

His wife was incredulous. 'Why ever for?'

'Um, as far as I know, it's something to do with the noise they make when they melt. The trapped air inside them escapes and, apparently, it sounds like an animal growling.'

'Oh, Lucien, you do know the strangest things.'

The husband turned his head slightly as if he could hear something. Glancing at his wife, who was still staring straight

77

ahead, he said, 'Dear me, I think I drank too much wine.'

Smiling, his wife nudged him playfully, 'Do you have a headache?'

He looked like he wasn't going to say anything but then changed his mind, 'No, no. It's just that … well, for a second there I thought I heard my Aunt Margaret. She used to have this incredible belly-wobbling laugh. Us children would make up jokes to tell her, to see who could get her going first.'

'Really, Lucien, you've never mentioned an aunt Margaret before.'

'Haven't I? Well, to be honest, I've not thought about her for years. I was barely ten when she died. For some reason I was her favourite. God bless her.'

Leaning in to kiss him on the cheek, his wife said, 'Then she must have had impeccable taste. I'm sure I would have liked her very much.'

'And I know she would have liked you too. Come on; let's get back inside. I'm literally going to die of the cold if we don't go inside this minute.'

I watched them head indoors, unsure whether to follow them or not. I suppose I had one thing to be grateful for, I couldn't feel the cold but, still, I certainly felt something in the air tonight. How lovely it would be to take off to the third-class communal room and watch the men's cheeks get brighter with every bottle of beer. Maybe there would be a singsong to help me forget all my troubles, whatever they were. Instead, however, for some reason I felt a strong urge to remain outside, and ready … for goodness knows what.

Suddenly I heard voices from way above me.

'Now, this is proper frosty, Fred. Ain't never felt this type of cold before.'

It was the lookouts, ninety feet above me, in the crow's-nest. I immediately headed up to them, glad of the company.

There were six lookouts altogether, all chosen because of their dedication and concentration. Theirs was a most important job. As the captain told them, they were the eyes of the ship. If they were the 'eyes' of *Titanic*, then that must mean that Harold and Jack, with the Marconi-transmitter, were her ears and even voice.

I never knew such a wonderful job existed – to be higher than anyone else onboard and be able to see for miles around. Had I known about it, I think I might have wanted to be a ship's lookout if I ever got bored with riveting. The 'nest' was one of my favourite places in *Titanic* and I did my best to be there to watch the sun both rise and set. It was only a small space to stand, just enough room for the two boys on duty, but what freedom they enjoyed from the rest of the staff and crew. On Captain Smith's ship, this isolated steel balcony was their own tiny island, to govern as they wished.

As usual, the more serious of these two, Frederick Fleet, was doing his best to ignore his colleague, Reggie, who never gave up trying to make conversation as he searched the sea ahead for obstacles.

'I can't see a blasted thing, can you?'

Fred mumbled something under his breath that neither Reggie nor I heard. Both their noses were running with the cold. Reggie sniffed loudly, making Frederick roll his eyes in annoyance.

'Ugh, it hurts to sniff. Wish I brought my handkerchief. Not long now, I suppose. Another thirty minutes or so. I could murder a cup of tea.'

It didn't seem to bother Reggie that his companion appeared to be completely ignoring him. He was a cheery lad who reminded me a little of the ever-smiling Jack from the shipyard, and he prattled on, 'You know, it seems strange to be doing this without binoculars. I mean, the daytime is one thing but, here, at night, it's different.'

At this, Frederick nodded, in spite of himself. I felt his anxiety, the tension in his back and neck, as he stared unblinking into the blackness. 'Can't believe there wasn't another key for the locker. You'd think with those ice warnings from the other ships that they'd just force the thing open, somehow,' he grumbled.

Reggie, showing no surprise in finally getting his partner to talk to him, wrapped his arms about himself. 'Ach, it wouldn't be so bad if there was a moon. Anyway, why are we worrying if the captain and the commanding officers aren't bothered? Sure, nothing could stop this ship, especially at this speed.'

Frederick shrugged, pushing his hands further into his coat pockets. 'That's what they say alright.'

It's a good name for it, the crow's-nest, because that's exactly what it felt like standing up here. It was a great deal higher than any height I had climbed with a boiling hot rivet. One could easily pretend to be a bird in flight, surveying the geography below him. The only sound to be heard was the faithful hum of the engine. As I stood behind the two boys, I could hardly hear or see the ocean around us. If I shut my eyes, I could easily convince myself I was anywhere at all.

Of course, working the dayshift was easier as long as there wasn't any mist or heavy rain. It struck me suddenly that the pleasure of this job would depend an awful lot on the weather. Fortunately, though freezing cold, tonight was dry. At least the chilly temperature prevented a tired lookout from dozing off.

The bridge was a few feet below us; this was where the ship

was steered. Officer Hitchens was at the wheel tonight with First Officer Murdoch at his shoulder. I had peeked in the window on my way up here. So, while the two lookouts weren't alone in their constant inspection of the miles in front of them – Officers Hitchens and Murdoch were doing their bit too – Fred and Reggie held the best position for spotting trouble. Captain Smith must have retired for the night. Idly I turned to catch the full view of *Titanic* behind us. It was a funny angle. From where we stood we had no appreciation of her size and majesty; she was simply too big to take in all at once, plus the view was blocked by the massive funnels.

I was so caught up in my thoughts that I barely noticed Fred bending sharply forward, craning his neck to see something. What was it? I hovered over his shoulder, reluctantly, hardly daring to make a proper effort to discover what had grabbed his attention and there, as I peered half-heartedly out into the darkness, something began to take shape in front of me. I looked at Fred in shock, completely forgetting that he couldn't meet my eye. Not allowing himself to blink, Fred gripped his companion's arm in stunned silence. Reggie obediently followed the direction of his mate's focus. I was already overwhelmed by sheer horror. It looked no bigger than a table, and then a table on top of another table, and then another and another, until there was no denying what we were facing. Ignoring Reggie's hushed swearing, Fred banged on the bell in the crow's-nest three times, as hard as he could, and then wrenched the phone receiver off its hook as the distance between the ship and the massive object shrank at an alarming rate. His call was answered immediately.

'What do you see?'

'Iceberg, sir, dead ahead.'

'Thank you.'

Fred clung to the rail in front of him, wishing it was the wheel and that he was able to take over the steering. All we could do was watch and wait – which is sometimes the hardest thing of all. No one said a word until we realised that Quartermaster Hitchens was attempting to turn the ship. What else was there to do but try? I'm sure that both he and Officer Murdoch were as breathless and as petrified as we were. The iceberg was so huge and far, far too near.

Fred was in agony, unable to stop himself from shouting out, 'Come on, *come on*. Go left ... LEFT!'

And she did start to turn. Reggie whistled as the immense size of the iceberg was made blatant. 'How did we not see that?'

It was a mountain of ice standing proudly up in the ocean, steep with sharp ridges that glistened dully beneath the stars.

Fred's reply was fierce, 'How *could* we have? We were both looking, weren't we? There's no moon in the sky and absolutely no wind, so there's no waves breaking against it, otherwise we'd have heard it, even if we couldn't see it.'

That was how a lookout usually spotted a berg at night; the sea warned him by slapping at it until the noise caught his attention. That night, however, the sea had been as still and silent as the iceberg itself.

'Plus,' offered Reggie, 'we were going really fast. They knew that icebergs were a possibility in this area, so you'd think they would've slowed down a bit.'

'Exactly,' said Fred.

Titanic's head continued ever so slowly to lean away from the obstacle.

'Yes, yes,' gasped Fred. 'Keep going.'

We were going to make it. It looked like we were going to make it, just about.

A collision couldn't be helped, perhaps, but it certainly could be reduced in size. So, it was that the ship clumsily skimmed the berg, resulting in the deck below us being showered by a brief avalanche of ice that had been torn free.

And that seemed to be it.

Fred and Reggie winked at one another, both presuming that there had been some sort of hit but neither completely sure, except for the bits of ice on the deck. They had neither heard nor felt the expected bang. Watching the iceberg disappear behind *Titanic*'s massive funnels, Reggie bumped against Fred, his face full of relief and gratitude.

'Phew! That was close, hey?'

I wasn't so sure.

As we had passed the iceberg, I'd felt *Titanic* shudder and then I'd heard what sounded to me like a groan. It reminded me of the low, brief sound that escaped my mother's lips when we heard that Da was gone – such a small, insignificant sound. I had no idea that it meant what it did – that she was destroyed forevermore.

Some passengers gathered on deck to inspect the chunks of ice, a few of the men kicking around one particular piece that was almost the size of a football.

Within a couple of minutes, I spied Captain Smith heading for the bridge and followed him, for the want of something better to do. It was obvious that there had been an event of some kind. Officer Hitchens' forehead was covered in sweat and it looked to me that his extra firm grip on the wheel was the only thing that was keeping him upright. Meanwhile, his commanding officer's face was pale and his breathing forced. Taking in the scene before him the captain seemed only a little bit curious.

'Good evening, gentlemen, has something happened? I thought I felt a slight lurch.'

Officer Murdoch looked relieved to see his boss. 'Sir, I think we've hit an iceberg.'

'I see. Well, you better have the carpenter make a quick tour, just in case. Call a halt in the meantime, until we get the all clear. And perhaps we'd better get hold of Thomas Andrews too – as fast as you can.'

'Aye, aye, Captain.'

With that, the engines were shut down, rendering *Titanic* lifeless – or so it seemed to me.

⚜ ⚜ ⚜

I didn't want to but I felt compelled to do a tour of my own. I could hear a strange sound that I assumed was coming from below. Taking my time, I passed through the different compartments. Not one person looked worried, although a few had noticed that the engines were mute. A woman in first class ventured out into the passageway and hailed a passing steward.

'Is there something wrong? Why ever have we stopped?'

The man was politely dismissive. His shift was over for the night and he was on his way back to his own quarters.

'I shouldn't worry, madam. The ship just hit an iceberg.

I'm sure we'll be on our way again in a few minutes. Good-night.'

The noise grew louder and louder as I made my way further into *Titanic*'s belly.

Down the steps I went to be almost run over, if that were possible, by the five postal workers. Each of them was one step behind the other, all tugging their own colossal bag overflowing with letters and packages. This was strange behaviour indeed, but the reason for it was made clear as soon as I entered the Mail Room. There was water, freezing green seawater spewing in through the wall. It was a terrifying sight. The sheets of metal that had been hammered into place by Charlie and Ed, using the rivets I had fetched and carried at great speed, had proved no match against the iceberg – the biggest, grandest, most powerful ship in the world had just been punctured by a block of frozen water.

And then, without meaning to, I suddenly found myself remembering a conversation that had taken place on the morning of the launch. At the time, of course, I thought it was nonsense, even comical. Ed was showing off his expert knowledge, as usual, pointing at the funnels and declaring, 'See how there's four of them, that's one more than any other ship, well, apart from her sister – and that's how you'd recognise her if you saw her again.'

Charlie, in a bid to change the subject, asked Ed about a rumour that was flying about the shipyard, 'Have you heard anything about cheap rivets? There's a story going around that we skimped on the rivets, or some of them, at any rate.'

We all stared at Charlie in disbelief, Jack and Ed in complete agreement for once.

'What on earth are you talking about?' Ed sounded as shocked as a vicar who had caught somebody telling rude jokes in church.

Charlie shrugged. 'I'm just repeating what I've heard: we ran out of the good rivets by the time we started working on the bow and the story is that cheaper ones were used.'

Ed shook his head and laughed. 'Charlie, for heaven's sake! This is Harland & Wolff, not some little amateur workshop, and that's the most important ship ever to be built. Do you really think they would have us using second-rate materials on her?'

⚜ ⚜ ⚜

'Hey buddy, we're flooding out down here. Could you give us a hand?'

A couple of stewards peeked down the stairs.

'Oh, my goodness! What's going on? Where's that water coming from?'

William, the American with the red, curly hair and spectacles, shrugged his round shoulders. 'We're not sure. Someone said something about hitting an iceberg.'

He grinned and nodded at Oscar, who was bravely struggling with a heavy load.

'We were celebrating Oscar's birthday when a guy told us that our room was flooding. Never even got to cut the cake; can you believe that?'

The stewards remained on the stairs but duly accepted a bag each. Like me they couldn't take their eyes of the water. One of them whistled softly. 'That's coming in fast.'

Neither Oscar nor his mates paid him any heed; so intent were they on emptying the wooden cubbyholes, shoving letters of all shapes and sizes into the bags. One of the Englishmen made it look like it actually hurt him to lump items meant for opposite destinations into the same bag. He glanced at William as he bunched together post for completely different districts in America. The American understood his reluctance but said, 'Forget about sorting, John. Our priority is to keep them dry. We'll sort them later.'

Chapter Seven

I had to find *Titanic*'s designer, Mr Andrews. He knew the ship better than anyone else. After  all, what could I know about these things? I was just a child. Maybe it was perfectly natural to have water flowing in at some point. And, anyway, nobody else looked as scared as I felt.

Mr Andrews met me on his way from the bridge. His face was expressionless, but he was walking much faster than he usually did. Just the sight of him calmed me and I was sure that whatever the problem was he would fix it. As he made his way downwards, everything seemed wonderfully normal. Gentlemen sat in the common rooms enjoying their cigarettes; couples lingered in corners enjoying private tête-à-têtes; and housekeeping staff flashed tired smiles of recognition as they finished up for the day. It was so very peaceful until, that is, he reached the engine room.

'Sir! Sir, she's letting in fast.'

It was as if we stepped into another world where panic was the order of the day. Fortunately there were no passengers around to eavesdrop. In Boiler Room 4 the men were pumping out the seawater and they seemed to be winning this particular battle too. However, I felt utter panic at the sight of so much water. Even Mr Andrews stopped sharply, his eyes wide in surprise. It was completely unexpected. Stokers, greasers, engineers, thoroughly drenched from head to toe, flew by to their various stations. Amongst the crowd was the Guarantee Group. Just like Quartermaster Hitchens, Roderick Chilsolm looked relieved to see his boss but also very worried.

'It's bad, sir. There's maybe ten feet of water in the first few compartments, where she took the side off herself. I'm not sure if it's a clean gash or the outer metal plates have buckled.'

Thomas nodded and asked, 'How many compartments?'

Roderick paused long enough for his boss's eyes to meet his before saying, 'Five in all, so far – at least.'

They approached another staircase, but there was no need to descend it fully. The corridor below was already running with water. Some letters were floating around; the ink on the envelopes had run making it impossible to read the names and addresses. Thomas noticed something else shimmering in the water. Roderick followed his gaze and leant down further down the steps. 'Someone's spectacles.'

Instinctively I went to hold Mr Andrew's hand, but, of course, I couldn't. The ship groaned as the three of us stood there. Or, I could almost swear it did. What was happening?

Mr Andrews face was filled with a sudden anguish. 'My God! All this time I've been worrying over the size of rooms while the bulk heads, the partition walls are too short.'

I didn't understand what he was talking about, but Roderick, who was studying his boss' face, understood immediately:

'As each compartment fills up to the brim with water it's spilling over the dividing wall into the next one.'

'Like dominoes,' whispered Thomas.

The two men looked at one another while I could only hang by in bewilderment. What were they saying? A brief nod passed between them and Thomas turned away, saying, 'Alright, then, I'd better go and tell Captain Smith.'

Roderick called after him,

'I'll be in the engine room if you need me.'

I went with Mr Andrews. His face remained expressionless, but I saw a tiny bead of sweat slide down his cheek. At least, I think that's what it was. The atmosphere around him felt heavy and I could sense him clamping down on an urge to run. All I could do was remain as close to him as I could. The walk back to the bridge seemed to take much longer than usual.

Captain Smith and First Officer Murdoch met him at the door and he beckoned them to step outside. For just a second the captain looked shocked, but Thomas pretended not to notice. He took a deep breath and kept his voice low: 'I'm afraid she's sinking. Five compartments are flooded. Two would have been fine; three would have given us much more time. Five, however, is utterly impossible.'

Neither of his listeners made any visible reaction, the captain merely asking, 'How much time do we have?'

'One hour, maybe two at the most.'

I don't know if I screamed. I think I might've opened my mouth but I wasn't sure if anything came out.

Neither the captain nor his officer moved a muscle. Thomas peered down the length of the ship. From where he stood he could see some of ship's sixteen lifeboats, more than any other ship had ever carried.

Almost to himself he nodded as he quietly declared, 'Of course, there aren't enough.'

The captain looked from the boats back to the designer and demanded, 'What are the numbers?'

Mr Andrews seemed a little dazed. 'These are Roderick Chisholm's boats – my chief draughtsman – his own design. Very fine boats indeed.'

The two officers glanced at one another. Officer Murdoch cleared his throat and said a little too loudly, 'Sir!' Mr Andrews suddenly came to and continued, 'They were tested in Belfast and can take up to 70 men in each. So, that's 1,120 seats all told. H … How many are on board?'

Captain Smith's reply was immediate, 'Including staff and crew, a little over two thousand.'

There was silence. Mr Andrews looked to *Titanic*'s captain, wanting, no doubt, to hear his solution while Officer Murdoch stared out into the darkness, also waiting for his captain to say something. In that moment, I understood how lonely it could be for a ship's captain, a prime minister, a president or even a king.

'Well then,' said the captain slowly, 'I'd better have the Marconi-boys summon all available ships to our rescue.'

Without waiting to hear his companions' reactions, he headed off, tugging the peak of his hat over his eyes.

Mr Andrews watched him go while Officer Murdoch called after him, 'Sir, should I have the crew informed, along with the passengers, and the lifeboats made ready?'

'Yes, yes … yes,' was the reply.

❖ ❖ ❖

I raced ahead of the captain to the Marconi-office, wanting to warn the two telegraphists but at a loss as to how to do that. As I entered the room, Jack appeared from the alcove, his hair sticking up at odd angles and his shirt creased from his collar to his belt. He must have been asleep. Harold was tapping out a message but stopped to ask his friend why he was awake. Jack answered with a question of his own, 'Why have the engines stopped?'

Harold removed the headphones and listened. 'Oh my goodness. You're right. I'm such a dolt, I never noticed a thing.'

Before they could pursue the matter further, the door opened and in walked Captain Smith, the last person they expected to see. Normally they brought his messages to him in the bridge room, while he sent his messages via his officers. The two operators stood to attention, to receive him. Captain Smith didn't bother with any trivial conversation.

'Good evening, gentlemen. We have a serious situation here. Fact is the ship has struck an iceberg and we have to evacuate. I need you to alert every other ship you can find and ask them to come to our aid immediately.'

It was incredible. This glorious ship, the biggest in the

whole wide world, the one that was 'practically unsinkable'; it didn't make any sense no matter how many times I heard it. She was only two short days into her very *first* voyage ever – and now she was sinking, in the middle of nowhere? So, she was never going to reach America, after all that work from all those men who had prepared her for a lifetime of service? Nobody else would ever get to see her. No! This wasn't right. What had it all been for? It didn't make any sense.

Wait a minute.

Was it a foreboding that I had felt all day long? Did I somehow know this was going to happen? Was that why I was here, to die all over again with *Titanic* by my side? Just like Captain Smith, I found myself turning to the tele-graphists, desperate for them to solve the appalling dilemma. *Titanic* needed help; people had to come and help us. There was no other way.

Harold, baffled by the unexpected instruction, let out an inappropriate, 'We've what?' but the captain was already on his way back to the bridge. Jack was the first to react and raced to the desk, gently pushing Harold aside. Grabbing the headphones, he started tapping, almost before he sat down, the special emergency code that signalled a ship in distress.

CMD. THIS IS TITANIC. WE HAVE STRUCK ICEBERG

SINKING FAST

COME TO OUR ASSISTANCE

Harold stood beside him, gripping the desk, his face a picture of pure bewilderment, as he muttered mostly to himself.

'Surely not? She's unsinkable. This can't be. An evacuation, an actual evacuation?'

Jack, preparing to send his message a second time, snapped at his friend, 'When was the last time Captain Smith paid us a personal visit?'

'Oh my God, you're right. I'll go outside and see what the situation is.'

In the five minutes Harold was gone, Jack sent the call for help over and over again. He worried that the operators on the other ships might have finished up for the night, switched off their machines and gone to bed. Praying that someone would answer him, he barely looked up at Harold's return. The latter's bewilderment had been replaced with a grave certainty.

'The passengers are being told to put on their lifejackets and make their way on deck where the lifeboats are being launched. Women and children first.'

He stopped to read what Jack was furiously writing. It was a message from the *Carpathia*:

WE ARE 58 MILES AWAY FROM YOUR POSITION AND ARE COMING HARD

Jack wrote down the particulars, *Carpathia*'s exact location, along with his educated guess that it would take them approximately four hours to reach them. Harold was mightily relieved.

'Phew, thank goodness for that. Well done, old boy.'

Without another word, he snatched up the note and shot out the door.

I stayed with Jack who was tapping out his relief and gratitude to *Carpathia*'s operator. Of course I knew more than the two boys did, but perhaps there had been fresh news that I wasn't aware off. Only a couple of minutes passed before Harold returned, looking pale and winded. I had hoped that I would be proved wrong; the truth was just too ridiculous. Naturally Jack was mystified and asked, 'What happened? Did you speak to the captain? What did he say?'

Running his hand through his hair, Harold faced his colleague. 'Yes, I saw him. I didn't even have to knock on the door; it was like he was waiting for one of us to appear. "Sir," I said, "it's the *Carpathia*. She's on her way, at full speed." I half thought he was going to hug me as he took your note.'

Jack was impatient, 'Yes, okay. Then what?'

Harold shook his head. 'He read the message and started

shouting at me, as if I was to blame.'

'What do you mean? To blame for what?'

Harold continued, 'He shouted and shouted, "NO! NO! This won't do at all. Four hours is too late. *She'll be gone by then.*"'

Jack put his head in his hands.

'Oh God, Jack, are you crying? Don't worry. There must be other ships out there that aren't so far away.'

Harold patted his colleague awkwardly on the shoulder.

'No, no, it's not that.'

Unable to look at Harold, Jack kept his hands over his face, 'Just before 8 o'clock tonight I was working like blazes, trying to get out as many messages as possible. You know, with the backlog.'

Harold's agreement was solid, 'Of course, there was a ton of stuff to send.'

'Yes, well, while I was in the middle of sending a detailed message about someone's new car, or something, I was blasted out of it by that youngster on the MV *Mesaba*. I swear he doesn't have a clue about what he's doing. He started going on about large numbers of icebergs and giving me the coordinates but since his message didn't begin with "MSG" I didn't think it was an official report for the captain. I thought he was just looking for a chat. So, I told him that I was too busy and to keep out.'

Harold pulled his friend's hands down. 'Come on, now. We've had, how many – five or six ice warnings over the forty-eight hours? This afternoon, when I brought another one to the bridge, Captain Smith told his man to shift our course by a few degrees. All those warnings had the MSG code and therefore we brought them to Captain Smith's attention immediately. That little twit knows the regulations just as well as the rest of us. And you know well that had he used the proper code you would have stopped what you were doing and taken it to the captain, allowing nothing to get in your way.'

Jack shrugged half-heartedly and said, 'Yes, I would've – of course I would've.'

'Okay, then. Let's see if we can find someone else as well as the *Carpathia*.'

Watching his friend straighten the headphones over his ears, Harold reminded him of something else, 'Don't forget, mate, if you hadn't insisted that we fixed the transmitter, we'd be in a right mess now.'

He received a watery smile in return before Jack put his head down and redoubled his efforts to find help.

Unfortunately it was too late for the five postal workers. For some reason I could see them clearly from the

Marconi-office. I was startled by the image of them floating about, bumping up gently against one another, looking as if they were only asleep. They must have ignored the rising water level to continue rescuing the post and then were suddenly overwhelmed. What a horrible birthday for poor Oscar – to drown on a ship. Nobody knew they were dead, only me. No doubt their families and friends were fast asleep, snug in their belief that they would see them again.

Of course my own father's body was never found, after that storm, when the sea took him and never gave him back. My mother was disinclined to believe he was gone and waited patiently for him to come through the front door, leaving it on the latch for him, day and night. When the vicar appeared on our doorstep, instead of Da, a few days later, to discuss funeral arrangements, she had the dog chase him up the street.

The smallness of the telegraphists' office was bothering me. I left the two boys behind and went out in search of something … what, I didn't know. To my surprise, I found that as soon as I focused on Mr Andrews I knew exactly where he was and made my way to him. He was in full flow, racing around, making sure everyone he met, staff and passenger, was wearing a bulky, milk-coloured lifejacket. Typically he was making no distinction between the little chambermaids and the first-class passengers that he met. One young girl went running past him and he immediately called after her, 'Annie, why aren't you wearing your lifejacket?'

The girl stopped confused and explained, 'Sorry, sir, it's just that the missus asked me to fetch her jewellery from the purser's office.'

I saw the impatience in his eyes before he quickly covered it up with a tight smile, and said firmly, 'Get your lifejacket before you get the jewels. Will you promise me that much?'

Annie nodded, 'Yes, sir. I'll go and get it right this minute.'

'That's my girl.'

She passed a foreman, one of the lower deck supervisors, as she headed off in the opposite direction. He was out of breath.

'Mr Andrews, I've been looking for you. I hear we're evacuating the passengers. How bad is it?'

The engineer glanced around to make sure they were alone and asked, 'Where are your men?'

'Some of them on duty in the boiler rooms while the rest of them, the day shift, are asleep in their dormitory.'

'I'm afraid it's as bad as can be, Harry. She's sinking fast – maybe an hour, maybe two, but no more than that. The best you can do is wake everyone up and get them into the lifejackets. Just keep it quiet, though, we don't want to start a panic just yet.'

With that, Mr Andrews strode off, leaving the man trembling in his wake. The man blessed himself quickly before galloping off towards his sleeping workers. Only, he wasn't alone. A young boy, even younger than me, was following him closely. I couldn't make out his features; in fact, I couldn't even be sure of what I was looking at. It was more like a blur or a silver shadow. The longer I stared after him, the less I could see.

It was too much to think about now. I just wanted to keep going. As I quickly moved through the different sections, I was surprised to find no signs of panic or upset. The staff, that is the staff who knew what was happening, remained tight-lipped and occupied in doing what they did best. I went outside to see what was going on. There, Commanding Officer Murdoch had all his officers line both sides of the deck, poised to start working the great pulleys that would release the white, wooden lifeboats down the side of *Titanic* to the sea, one at a time. The crew, for the most part, knew what they were doing, so there was only the passengers' confusion to deal with – which was no small thing.

There was a group of passengers on deck, all from first class, and they seemed more annoyed than worried about the whole situation. There was a lot of stamping of feet and exclamations about the cold weather. All of them were squashed into their lifejackets and not many were too pleased about it. One woman called out to the officer who had been put in charge of the first lifeboat, 'Must we wear this awful thing? It's extremely uncomfortable.'

I recognised her as one of the posh ladies from the captain's dinner table. She stood in between her husband and the young woman who I guessed, from her plain dress, to be her maid.

The young officer looked slightly unsure of himself, 'I'm sorry, madam, but Captain said everyone is to put on a lifejacket.'

She refused to be satisfied with this, however, and looked as if she suspected the officer of lying to her.

'Where is the captain? I wish to speak to him immediately.'

Suddenly Officer Murdoch appeared and answered her brusquely, 'I'm afraid Captain Smith is rather busy at the moment.'

Before she could make a reply to this, he turned to address the sulky gathering:

'Ladies and gentlemen, if I could have your attention, please. We are ordered to evacuate the ship and therefore will be lowering the first of the lifeboats within the next few minutes. Could I ask all the ladies and children to step forward as they will be lifted out first?'

There was a standoff between the freezing passengers and officers. I couldn't believe it; not one woman made a single move. Instead, a man in a shiny top hat tut-tutted crossly, 'I say, is this really necessary? Surely it's a bit melodramatic. I mean, where is the captain? Shouldn't he be talking to us?'

Officer Murdoch, to his credit, didn't seem very surprised by the crowd's reaction. The same couldn't be said of his colleagues who were standing off to the side. They caught each other's eyes and carefully made faces of disbelief to one another. I must admit to finding it all funny, in a tragic sort of way. The captain's word is law on a ship, but what happens when some of the richest people in the world refuse to carry out his orders.

When Officer Murdoch caught several women sending spiteful glances towards the less than glamorous lifeboat, he took a guess as to what the problem might be.

'I assure you, ladies, you will be quite safe. Once you have all taken your seats, my men and I will let the boat down very slowly. It is a long way down, I grant you, but perhaps it would be better if you kept your eyes closed, until you reached the water.'

For the benefit of the men, he added, 'The captain insists.'

Still the passengers remained unimpressed with the proceedings.

One lady, wrapped up in fur, took her husband's arm and turned away, saying, 'Let us go back inside, my dear. We will be far safer on this ship than sitting in the middle of the ocean on that little thing and a great deal warmer too.'

Most of the crowd seemed to agree with the woman and shuffled back inside. However, much to everyone's surprise, including mine, the complaining couple and their maid remained where they were. Maybe it was because they had wisely put on their heavy coats or maybe it was because they liked the captain so much – whatever it was, it was enough. The haughty lady addressed the officers loudly and clearly, 'Very well, then. I'll get into your boat but I absolutely insist that my husband comes with me.'

As far as I could see, Officer Murdoch had no choice. For one thing, there was no reason not to let the stern-looking gentleman take a seat, since there was hardly any other competition for it. More importantly, time was ticking by and, in order to encourage the rest of the passengers to make a move, Officer Murdoch needed someone to get into the first lifeboat, so that the rest would follow by example. After all, there were fifteen other boats to get started on. He nodded to the young officer to let them through. Relieved to be in charge once again, the young man gestured at his fellow sailors and they re-assumed their positions at the pulley.

'Very good, madam. Give me your hand and watch your step.'

Suddenly there was a bit of a commotion.

'Here, here, let us through, there's a good chap.'

It was the chief baker, Charles Joughin, with four loaves of bread in his arms. He appeared to be leading a small army of fellow bakers, all carrying four loaves each.

'All right, boys, take a boat each and deposit your bread – careful mind. Don't let them get bashed.'

Charles gazed after his assistants with pride, and seemed to address the backs of the snooty husband and wife, since they wouldn't trouble themselves to turn around, or maybe it was just their pretty maid that he made his excuses to. 'That's my pantry cleared out, forty pounds of bread. I was going to bring some cakes, but I thought they'd be too messy, you know with the cream and that. Anyway, here you are then.'

With that, he passed the bread over to the maid who had been doing her best to follow her mistress into the boat. 'Oh … well I … er, thank you.'

Luckily one of the officers, who could hardly hold in his laughter, was able to take the bread from her otherwise she would have been stuck as she definitely needed both hands to climb over the side of the boat – and neither the Lord nor Lady appeared willing to help her.

Beaming with satisfaction, the baker headed back inside. I decided to follow him. At the door of the busy first-class lounge he met Wallace Hartley with his band of musicians and exclaimed, 'Ah, Wallace, we meet again. And these must be your good friends. How do you do, gentlemen?'

I was struck by the fact that the musicians were all wearing their coats and clutching their instruments at the ready – except for the man who played the piano.

'Charles! We're in a bit of a rush, I'm afraid, but I might as well introduce you to everyone while we're here. This is Jock, Theodore, Fred and Roger. Lads, this is Mr Charles Joughin, Chief Baker.'

Everyone shook hands.

'Where are you all off to, do you have a boat to catch?'

Wallace laughed and replied, 'Gosh, no. Captain Smith asked us to go outside to play to the passengers while they're being evacuated – just to keep things cheerful like.'

Charles was delighted. 'What a wonderful idea. I think the ladies, especially, probably need a bit of comforting alright. Music always makes me feel a lot better about things – and if I can't have music, I'll take whiskey instead.'

Theodore held the door open for his friends and said, 'Well, Charles, it was lovely to meet you. Will you be coming out to listen to us?'

'Oh, I'll be along presently, I'm sure. I think I'll just take care of a few things first. If you know what I mean,' the baker replied with a wink.

Again everyone laughed and shook the baker's hand again as they all trooped outside. Charles couldn't resist calling after them, 'Don't forget to play my favourite song!'

He made his way back downstairs with me close behind. I was intrigued about the things he wanted to take care of. A few minutes later we were in his quarters. There was no sign of the other bakers that he shared his room with. The cabin was warm and cosy, betraying no hint of the freezing temperatures outside. Reaching into his bag, he pulled out a half bottle of whiskey.

'Hello, my lovely.'

I couldn't believe it.

Stretching himself out on his narrow bed, he casually bunched up his pillow into the back of his neck, so that he could drink in a horizontal position. Humming his favourite song about the seaside, he slowly unscrewed the top of the bottle and took a mouthful of the brown liquid.

He was the picture of a contented man. 'Glorious, just

glorious! Exactly what the doctor ordered, at a time like this.'

As he took a second mouthful, there was a burst of shouting in the distance. He barely raised an eyebrow and merely took a third sip. On his fifth sip he began a conversation, 'Well, I don't know what's to become of us but I tell you one thing for nothing; I'm not going to panic. Nope, it's all going to work out just fine. Everything always does in the end.'

He took another large mouthful. I sat at the end of his bed, pretending he was talking to me.

'The thing is, as Nana Joughin – may God rest her soul – always said, the less worrying a person does allows their problems to fix themselves naturally, in their own good time.'

With that he put the top back on the bottle, and laid it gently beside him, flattening out his pillow to allow himself to recline perfectly.

'Ah, Nana, you were the finest of women. I hope you're having a fine old time up there, wrestling with Saint Peter and joking with the Good Lord himself. God bless you. Sure, I might be seeing you soon.'

Then, bellowing out a contented yawn, he shut his eyes and floated off to sleep.

Chapter Eight

Leaving the baker to his dreams, I sped down to third class. Just as I suspected, Jim, Isobel and the children were still fast asleep. I couldn't help smiling, in spite of everything, when I heard baby Sarah snoring louder than her father. The scene was the same from cabin to cabin. Hundreds below deck had no idea that anything was amiss. After all, there were so many doors to be knocked on, starting with the wealthiest. It was really frustrating, even if I could have caused some commotion by sending something crashing to the ground, to wake up them up, there was absolutely nothing in the tiny cabin aside from the beds and wash basin, and they were all firmly nailed into place. I tried blowing on Jim's face, but he merely scratched his nose as he slept. There was nothing for it but to trust that the efficient and hard-working staff would be along shortly to get everybody up. With some reluctance I took a last look at the contented family, promising them that I'd be back as soon as I could.

I went back up on deck to scan the black sea in the hope of spying an approaching ship. Maybe Charles was right, that it would all work out in the end. I hadn't visited the Marconi-office in a while. For all I knew they could have contacted someone who could help us in time. However, there was nothing on the horizon – nothing around *Titanic* except cold water, ice and more ice.

Frederick Fleet and his fellow lookout Reggie looked stunned by all the activity on deck. I saw them shyly approach Officer Murdoch and present themselves for duty. Reggie was sent one way while Frederick was sent another.

'Okay, Fleet, go over and make yourself useful to Officer Lightoller.'

Frederick made his way to the other side of the deck, keeping his eyes down the whole time. It was as if he was somehow scared of the passengers around him. In fact, there wasn't a sadder face to be seen. I watched him take a deep breath as he stepped up to the broad figure of Officer Lightoller, and I felt prompted to stand beside him for he seemed in dire need of a friend.

Officer Lightoller was a tough-looking sailor, with square shoulders and a wide-legged stance. I wouldn't have been at all surprised to find he was some sort of boxing champion. He wasn't as polite as his colleagues, being far more concerned with carrying out his job as efficiently as possible and allowing no one to stand in his way. Therefore, when a well-dressed lady, upon being beckoned forward by him, shook her head violently and began to cry, she found herself being grabbed by Lightoller's assistants and practically tossed into the lifeboat. He'd probably have treated his grandmother in the exact same way. Really, I couldn't help admiring the officer who seemed completely unafraid of crying women and the upper classes.

'Sir, Frederick Fleet reporting for duty, sir, on Officer Murdoch's orders.'

'Very good, Fleet. You're one of the lookouts, aren't you? This one is just about ready to be set down, so I need you on it. I trust you can row a boat.'

Fred opened his mouth to make a reply but Lightoller rushed on.

'Well, if you don't, you'll soon learn. Take the right oar. Two other men will go with you, to help row and navigate.'

'Yes, sir.'

They watched a young girl and her anxious mother thread their way into the boat. Fred took the opportunity to ask his new commanding officer a question.

'Sir, where should we row to?'

Keeping his eye on the mother and daughter, the officer replied in a low voice, 'Just row as fast as possible away from the ship. After that, your navigator is in charge.'

Fred managed to hide the gulp of fear he inhaled, from Lightoller, at least. *So, that was it.* Titanic *was going to sink.* That's why Lightoller told him to row fast, in case the lifeboat got pulled down into the ocean with her.

Whereas I was perfectly free to be upset and confused, the young lookout was losing a battle to control his emotions. I felt his panicked embarrassment when his disobedient eyes misted over with tears. Lightoller, who had shown no patience for sobbing women, seemed mostly curious about the tearful boy standing beside him.

'Whatever is the matter? You're going to be safe. Apart from having to deal with that lot, you're going to be fine.'

Fred blinked hard.

'It's ... it's not that, sir. It was me that saw the iceberg; only I saw it too late, didn't I? This is all my fault. I looked and looked, but we were almost on top of it before I could make it out.'

Like me, the older man was genuinely struck by the sorrow on the lookout's face. Glancing around to make sure he was free to say what he wanted, he gestured at Fred to move closer.

'Fleet, I'll tell you something but don't repeat it to anyone else, alright? You're not to blame for this. Maybe no one person is. Having said that, one thing I'd have done differently is this: I'd have let her hit that blooming iceberg head on. As far as I'm concerned, none of this would be happening if she had just smashed her nose into it.'

With that, Officer Lightoller turned away to issue orders for the boat to be lowered. For the last time he called for more women and children, but none came forward. There were other boats waiting to be launched, so it was time to move on. Fred understood the conversation was over and readied himself for action.

The women in the boat were like sheep. They sat demurely, hands by their side, in silence, without the slightest idea of what to expect next – except for one. It was the forthright American, Mrs Brown, another diner from Captain Smith's table. She was looking at Frederick, with some concern, obviously noting the fact that he was far from happy. As the young boy accidentally met her eye, she startled him by winking mischievously. It was strange how such an observant woman didn't notice that her wide-brimmed hat, which was over loaded with flowers and ribbons, kept knocking the head of the tense-looking woman sitting beside her.

Lightoller gestured to the boat.

'Off you go then, Fleet. Don't forget, right oar with long, even strokes.

Fred climbed in and took the seat on the starboard side, gripping the large, wooden oar with both hands, despite the fact it would take several minutes to make the long descent to the water below. I was interested to see the descent. There were a few gasps from the women as the boat swayed in mid-air, inching its way down the side of the enormous ship. Mrs Brown, probably attempting to offer comfort, said loudly, 'Well, girls, thank goodness it isn't windy. Imagine doing this in the middle of a storm.' No one answered her, but she didn't seem to mind.

At least the journey to the ocean was well-lit. All the windows and port-holes blazed with light. No doubt the ladies found it peculiar to be that close to the outside of a ship. Of course, it was a position I was very familiar with. A few of the women were also in terror at being so high in the air. They shut their eyes tightly, one of them mouthing the words of a prayer.

One young girl, sitting in front of Frederick, slowly leant towards the edge of the boat. Mrs Brown immediately called out to her, 'No, honey. Don't look down. It will only upset you, and it's probably best not to look up either.'

I could see Frederick discreetly straining to see as much of

116

Titanic as possible. He was doing his best not to draw attention to himself, especially from the flamboyant American. I guessed him to be searching for any visible evidence of the collision with the iceberg. The puzzled look on his face told me that he couldn't see anything out of the ordinary. When they eventually sat on the water, the other sailor told Fred to follow his lead, waiting a heartbeat before plunging his oar into the sea. Fred did the same.

Both rowers were facing the ship in order to row away from her. As I watched, Fred did a double-take. He was staring at the front of the ship. Next I saw him glance cautiously at his neighbour, who gave him a warning look, indicating that he should keep quiet and continue rowing. How I wished I could see what they did. Within a couple of minutes, they had disappeared into the silent, dark night and I found myself glad to turn back to the noisy, crowded deck once more.

Wallace and his band were playing lively music that I didn't recognise. I thought it made a huge difference to hear the cello and the violins singing out such a catchy tune. Not many people seemed to be really listening to them, yet quite a crowd had gathered near them. The officers were working hard to fill the lifeboats and then launch them, though they still faced resistance from a lot of the passengers. I found a tense Thomas Andrews walking the length of the ship, interrupting the clusters of women who were standing around talking instead of climbing into the lifeboats.

'Ladies, you must get in at once. There isn't a moment to lose. You haven't time to pick and choose your boat. Don't hesitate. Please, get in. Get in.'

It bothered me that none of the launched lifeboats was actually full. For instance, that first boat containing the grand couple and their maid had just twelve people in it. There should have been seventy, not twelve. What madness! Mr Andrews joined me at the railings, checking perhaps to see how the boats sat on the water. 'Oh, my God!' he mumbled to himself, before calling to one of the sailors, 'Why aren't those boats filled to their proper capacity?'

'Because they won't bloomin' get in them,' was the rude reply. The busy man obviously didn't know who he was talking to.

Pain was etched across the engineer's face as he rushed to the nearest group of people and pleaded, 'Ladies, I must insist on you leaving *immediately*.'

Just then there was an explosion in the sky above us, a flash of colour dashing forth for just an instant. A few of the women screamed.

Mr Andrews called out, 'Don't be alarmed; they've set off the rockets to alert ships to our situation.'

At this explanation, there was a huge shift in the passengers' attitudes. Up to that point, the majority had trouble accepting that the evacuation was an absolute necessity. Scenes of utter disbelief were played out, from one side of *Titanic* to the other.

'Must I really get into that tiny thing? I thought this ship was unsinkable. Where's the captain? I demand to see him.'

and

'Do you really expect us to believe that a ship of this size and magnitude is going to sink because of some iceberg?'

These same voices were instantly silenced by the whooshing sound of the first rocket. Nobody could argue with the fact that a ship releasing rockets was a ship in distress. Hundreds of husbands, fathers, brothers and sons now turned to their womenfolk and bade them to go. Very few women, however, were immediately obedient. In many cases crewmen were forced to drag women away from their male companions, turning deaf ears to the screams of protest. Here and there some of the men tried to convince their families that they would be following on a later boat.

One elderly couple caught my eye. They were standing in the centre of a small circle of gentlemen, who seemed to know them well, and reminded me of my father's parents – grey and dignified in their obvious devotion to one another.

'Mrs Strauss, there is no need to be afraid. You will be perfectly safe, as will Mr Strauss. We won't leave his side.'

His wife smiled vaguely at her friends but didn't budge an inch.

The gentleman, Mr Strauss, gently remonstrated with his wife for not obeying the captain's orders.

'Rosalie, Captain Smith wishes you to get into a lifeboat, along with the other women and children.'

However, Mrs Strauss only pursed her lips and kept a hold on her husband's arm. I'm sure that the old man could have made her go had he issued her with a stern order, but something prevented him from taking this final step. I sensed his reluctance to say goodbye to her. One of the men tried a different line of reasoning.

'Madam, with all respect, if you don't go Mr Strauss will be anxious about your safety. Surely you don't want to cause him undue worry.'

It seemed she had finally been convinced. Hanging her head, she mumbled, 'Very well, Isidor,' and allowed herself to be escorted to join the line of women and children waiting to board Lifeboat Number 8. However, when her husband stepped away from her to rejoin his friends, she flipped around to look at him. How small and vulnerable he must have seemed to her as he took his place beside the taller, younger, and altogether stronger-looking men. No doubt she was thinking about the fact that she had taken care of them both for many years and now, *here we are in this dreadful situation, from which I am expected to just waltz off and leave him behind.* I wasn't the least bit surprised when she shook her head and marched right back to her group. Ignoring the crowd, the harassed officers and the worried frowns of their companions, she looked her husband in the eye and stated firmly, 'We have been married for over forty years. Where you go, I go.'

Her husband knew better than to waste any more time in persuading her to leave again. Besides, I think he preferred that they be together, no matter what. Some of the young gentlemen came up with a different plan. One of them gestured to Mr Strauss and then to the lifeboat, saying, 'I'm sure nobody would mind a gentleman of your years getting in and then you could both be safe.'

But the old man wouldn't hear of it. 'No, I will not go before other men.'

Likewise, his wife didn't bother arguing with him. Their decision made, to face whatever was coming, side by side, they smiled at one another and walked away from their companions, hand in hand, to the deckchairs to take a seat.

'No, Lucien, I can't. I'm not leaving you.' It was the same

couple I had spied earlier, when the husband thought he heard the laughter of his favourite aunt.

The wife was crying as her husband led her by the hand towards the officer who was calling for more women and children. Fixing his face into a stern expression, he took a deep breath and turned to her, dropping her hand as if in annoyance – but I knew he didn't mean it.

'I never expected to have to ask you to obey me, but this is one time you must. My dear, it's only a matter of form to have women and children first. The ship is thoroughly equipped and everyone on her will be saved.'

She was obviously unused to having him speak to her like that and bowed her head in shame. Her nose had begun to run in the cold air, and since all her belongings were back in their cabin she quickly dabbed at it with the sleeve of her coat. Lucien, a dark, handsome man with a kind face, placed his own handkerchief into her trembling hands and firmly turned her by the shoulders, so that she had but one step further to take before being helped into the lifeboat. Looking miserable, she took her place in the middle of the strangers. None of the other women was in a position to offer her much sympathy as they were much too worried about the men on deck waving them a fond farewell. Lucien, knowing only his wife, stepped back, utterly alone, into the shadows, so that she wouldn't see his own tears.

A scuffle broke out beside us. An old lady, with grey hair and huge bosoms, was actually fighting off the two officers who were trying to force her into the lifeboat. I couldn't see any man with her, husband or otherwise, as she punched out with her fist of jewellery, screeching at the top of her voice, 'Leave me alone, you brutes. I am not getting into that bath-tub. How dare you! Take your filthy hands off me.'

I could plainly see the terror in her eyes and, finally, her captors, realising that there were still hundreds of women and children who *wanted* to be saved, let her go. She took off at an impressive speed, heading for goodness knows where. Lucien saw all of this and was filled with a new appreciation for his brave wife. As her boat was being lowered, he raced to the edge of the deck and called after her, 'Maria, Maria. Be brave. Everything will be fine. See you soon, my love.'

What a difference his words made. Her tear-stained face lit up with pure joy as she blew him a kiss to show him that she wasn't afraid any more. She would be brave, just for him, just as he asked.

Chapter Nine

I fled to the Marconi-room, hoping to hear some good news. Jack was now in communication with several other ships. Harold arrived in just behind me, and asked him for an update.

'Well, *Titanic*'s sister, the *Olympic*, is rushing to meet us, but she's even farther away than the *Carpathia*. There are a few ships heading in our direction, but not one is close enough.'

Jack's voice cracked slightly but he covered it up with a cough.

'What's happening upstairs?'

Not wanting to add to his friend's stress, Harold kept his answer vague, 'Oh, it's mad busy. The band is playing, though, which is a nice touch. All the toffs are moaning about the cold, as if the staff could do anything about that.'

'Do you think the passengers know the truth about ... well, everything?'

Harold shrugged and replied, 'No, or at least I don't think so. I heard that Mr Andrews was the only one telling them that there wasn't any time to lose. I suppose it wouldn't help to start an all out panic. Besides, Jack, I heard one of the officers tell his mate that the ship couldn't sink. He said she was her own lifeboat.'

'Oh, right,' said Jack. He gave Harold a strange look.

Harold in turn looked genuinely puzzled and asked, 'What? That's great, isn't it?'

Moving a pile of papers around his desk, Jack said, 'It would be even better had it come from Mr Andrews.'

I stayed with them a while. To be honest, the scenes on deck involving families being split in two were exhausting me. I felt myself utterly swamped by all the sadness and the fear until I couldn't think straight. Meanwhile here, in this snug tiny office, business went on as usual. Jack tapped out messages over and over again while Harold sat by quietly, waiting for that one piece of good news that he could bring back to Captain Smith. These two boys knew exactly how things stood and yet they didn't lose hope for an instant. Both of them kept a quiet eye on the clock overhead. It was now 1.25 in the morning.

Jack sighed, 'I'm trying not to block the one line we have, so I'm keeping the messages as short as possible, but I think this is preventing the other operators from grasping the seriousness of the situation.'

As if to demonstrate his point, the *Olympic* sent a blissfully naive question.

ARE YOU STEERING SOUTH TO MEET US?

Jack took a second to work out how best to answer the query, to communicate in just one sentence that *Titanic* was in such a bad way that she was no longer sailing, that she was actually sinking on the spot.

WE ARE PUTTING THE WOMEN OFF IN THE BOATS

The next onslaught of bleeping was a question from a ship called the *Frankfurt* that was also miles away.

ARE THERE ANY SHIPS AROUND YOU ALREADY?

Harold jumped as Jack let out an exasperated shout, 'Oh, for heaven's sake! What a stupid question. Would I still be tapping away here if I didn't need their blooming help?'

'Just ignore them,' suggested Harold. 'They're much too far away anyway.'

Bewilderment was etched all over Jack's features as he said, 'I can't believe that there is no one else.'

'Hey, I know,' said Harold. 'Instead of the CQD, why don't you use the new code, the SOS. See if it brings us any luck.' He winked at his worried friend. 'You never know, this could be your last time to try it out.' To his relief, Jack laughed a little, in spite of himself.

The operator on the *Frankfurt* was obviously feeling hard done by and sent through a second message.

WHAT'S UP OLD MAN?

Almost beside himself with rage, Jack raced off a reply, his index finger tapping out one line that meant a whole lot more.

YOU FOOL. STAND BY AND KEEP OUT.

It worked. Not another beep was heard from that particular ship.

⚜ ⚜ ⚜

Hearing Thomas Andrews' voice in the distance, I took my leave of the wireless operators. It wasn't right of me to hide away like that, only I did so want to be present for any news of an approaching ship. He was hurrying downwards and I felt his need to suppress all the confusion he was feeling. Somehow I glimpsed, in his mind's eye, a picture of his wife and baby daughter. Running a hand across his shiny forehead he said aloud, to himself, me and this long corridor of *Titanic*, 'If I start feeling sorry for myself now, then I'm no good for anyone.'

We passed two young bellboys who saluted Mr Andrews.

'Boys, if anyone is looking for me, I'm just going down to the engine room. And please put on your lifejackets. That is an order!'

I don't know what he was expecting to find, but he certainly seemed surprised to open the door of the engine room and discover his fellow engineers, team of joiners, electricians and plumbers, including the entire Guarantee Group. The young Belfast boys seemed positively delighted to be a part of the busy crowd.

'Goodness! What are you all doing here?'

Roderick stepped forward. 'Keeping her going, sir.'

Mr Andrews looked around at the faces of the engineers and electricians, who calmly met his gaze in turn. They all knew the truth of the situation; he had made sure of that. The noise in the room was fierce as the massive engines continued to churn on, oblivious to the emotion that filled many eyes with the barest hint of tears. I could hear Mr Andrews' thoughts once more, *What a true privilege it is to know these men and boys.*

He had always been the kind of man who preferred to see

the good in everyone he met. Sometimes he was rewarded for his optimism and sometimes he wasn't, but he never gave up expecting all people to be good at heart. Swallowing a lump in his throat, he asked Roderick how long they were going to stay. Most of the men were standing in water, maybe an inch or more. The youngest of the boys had tucked the ends of their trousers into their socks.

The supervisor glanced around his companions who nodded to him in agreement. He smiled and shrugged at his boss, suddenly shy. 'Well, as long as it takes, sir. I mean, we can't have the heat or the lights going out; it would only scare the passengers, especially the kiddies.'

Mr Andrews replied in a strained voice, 'Yes, I see. Very good, then.'

With that, Roderick called out, 'All right, lads, let's get back to work.'

As Thomas turned to leave, a few of the men wished him a good night.

For a few seconds I was tempted to stay behind, in the hope that I could be of help in some way. The energy in the room seemed to be pulsating. Maybe it was the camaraderie among these brave work colleagues or maybe it was because here was the source of *Titanic*'s power. As I dithered over what to do, whether to stay or go, I suddenly sensed that the men weren't alone. Little flashes of white light danced in and around the workers unchecked.

Next I noticed Ennis, one of the youngest apprentices, peering in wonder at a particular bunch of wires and switches. His supervisor, William Parr, joined him to see what he was looking at. The apprentice glanced around, almost apologetically.

'This shouldn't be working. I mean, it had stopped working a few hours ago. The fuse had blown and I was just going to replace it now. But it's working again.'

William shrugged, 'Maybe there was nothing wrong with it in the first place.'

Ennis rubbed the area around the switch, making sure it was free of sea water, 'Maybe ...'

Seeing that the boy wasn't convinced, William tried again, 'Or maybe your guardian angel is an electrician?'

They both laughed and, as they did, I swear I could see a glow around them. In that moment I felt released from my need, or sense of obligation, to stay. I hurried after Mr Andrews, not stopping to ask myself any questions.

Just as I caught up with the engineer, he rounded a corner and almost collided with Captain Smith. Both men eyed each other warily. I had been wondering what had happened to the captain and I felt Mr Andrews wanting to ask him where he had been for the last while. I was pretty sure that neither realised the horrific guilt the other was feeling. The corridor was full of unspoken words and stifled emotions while the captain tried to look merely irritated at this unexpected meeting.

An awkward silence was broken by Mr Andrews. 'Is there any more news from other ships?'

The captain stared past him as he made a reluctant negative reply, '*Carpathia* is still over two hours away, maybe three.'

Neither captain nor designer was wearing a lifejacket, a fact that escaped them both.

'I've just been to the engine room.' Thomas smiled sadly as he spoke. 'All of them – the whole thirty-four of them – refuse to leave.' He looked down at the captain's feet. 'They said they didn't want the lights going out and frightening the passengers.'

As if to himself, he continued on talking but in a quieter tone, 'Half of them have wives and children while the other half are mere boys still living at home with their parents. Husbands, fathers, sons, all prepared to work together until the end. Quite wonderful, really.' He looked up again at the captain. 'Don't you think?'

Captain Smith was unwilling to pursue this line of

conversation and cleared his throat nervously before speaking, 'Actually, I was just on my way down there to check out the situation.'

Thomas shrugged, almost dismissively, 'Well, there's water in the engine room now.'

The two men had nothing more to say. Things were as bad as they could be, for another while at least. They parted in silence. This time I remained with the captain as he watched Mr Andrews disappear from sight. Once we were alone, he took off in the direction of the Marconi-room, where he entered without knocking.

'Is there any more news to be had?'

'No, sir,' replied Harold, as Jack watched uneasily from his chair.

The grey-haired man nodded as if he had heard exactly what he expected to.

'Righto. Well, I'm just letting you both know that water has reached the engine room.' Here, the captain took a moment after hearing a slight wobble in his voice. 'I'm sure you both know what this means. The power can't last much longer. When the water reaches the wires, the electrical boards will short circuit.' Breathing heavily he paused for a second. 'Which means the end to the lights, heat and, of course, your machine'

On delivering this gloomy summary, he left, and Jack started frantically tapping out a new message to the operator on the SS *Carpathia*:

COME AS QUICKLY AS POSSIBLE
ENGINE ROOM IS FILLING UP TO THE BOILERS

⚜ ⚜ ⚜

The baker woke up suddenly, in surprise. I had decided to check in on him, having forgotten about him for a while.

'Who's there? What was that noise?'

Of course I was unable to answer him.

He rubbed his eyes for a few seconds, looking like he might just go back to sleep. This I couldn't allow him to do. The scene had changed much since my previous visit. Fortunately, though, he heaved himself up on his elbows, glancing at his watch as he did so.

'Cripes! How long have I been asleep anyway? Don't tell me I'm late for work!'

He sat up and swung his feet out confidently to rest them on the floor, where he was utterly bewildered to hear what sounded like a splash. The sound was instantly followed by the sensation of water pooling around his ankles and seeping into his flimsy work shoes. Charles stared in puzzlement at his feet, as if they belonged to someone else. It took at least half a minute before he remembered.

'Aha, iceberg; all passengers leaving on lifeboats. Well, I never. So, they weren't exaggerating.'

The almost empty whiskey bottle lolled quietly nearby, on its side. It must have fallen off the bed and caused the noise which woke him. The liquid inside the bottle looked like it was doing its best to meet with the liquid outside. It chased its way around as the bottle turned this way and that. Delighted to see his old friend, Charles reached for it and took a small sip, just to help him wake up properly and decide what to do next. He took another sip, to be sure, tapping his feet against the ground to see if he could create a little wave.

Something caught his eye in the water. Charles bent over to get a closer look. It was a small, black spider that was losing the struggle to find dry land. The baker, who was instinctively, I felt, a rather compassionate man, scooped the weary creature up in his large hand. The rescued spider stood still, as if trying to catch its breath, allowing both it and its rescuer to size one another up. Lifting his outstretched hand closer to his face, the baker addressed the soaked creature in a kindly manner.

'You poor little mite. Just take a minute there to dry yourself.'

The spider didn't move a muscle, despite Charles looking off into the distance, respecting, as it were, the spider's privacy should it indeed wish to grab a towel and dry itself off. I watched, fascinated, welcoming a break from worrying about *Titanic*'s possible treacherous future.

I had always taken a great interest in the world of small creatures, especially during those lonely days before I joined Harland & Wolff. In fact, it proved a great way to forget, however briefly, both about my lack of human friends and Da. It was my first important discovery, that there were hundreds of daily adventures taking place in the same dull, sad house I shared with my mother.

One time I watched fascinated as a wasp tried to free itself from a spider's web. Guiltily I thought about helping it but didn't see how I could do this without getting stung. My guilt vanished, however, when the web's owner shot out of its dark corner and picked its way leisurely across the threads, to see what he had caught. The wasp had nothing to worry about. The spider was half its size and no one realised this faster than the spider which was being rocked violently from the vibrations caused by the enraged wasp. Nervously, or so it seemed to me, the spider stuck out a leg, to get an approximate measure of the intruder. He did it twice, as if to be completely sure. The wasp feeling itself to be gently 'felt' doubled his exertions to free himself, beating his wings so fast that I couldn't see them.

Then the strangest thing happened. Or maybe it wasn't so strange at all, since I had wondered how on earth the little spider was going to subdue an aggressive creature that clearly outweighed him. The spider returned to his corner to, I thought, consider his options. Meanwhile, the wasp freed one leg, only to get it immediately entangled again. Would the spider wait until the wasp had exhausted itself and then move in to take him? Could wasps sting spiders? Would the sting kill the spider? In the end none of my questions were answered, because the spider did something much more sensible. Cautiously he retraced his steps to just above where the wasp was stuck and began to pick apart the threads, one by one. The clever creature was helping the wasp to escape, thereby saving his web and himself a whole lot of trouble. Unable to fly off immediately, the wasp dropped to the window sill, slightly dazed. I couldn't imagine that it would taste very nice anyway and I admired the spider for keeping a cool head throughout.

With my thoughts miles – and years – away in Belfast, I had almost forgotten where I was until the baker suddenly reminded me by loudly exclaiming, 'Wait! Don't I know you? Aren't you the one that made that dainty web above my bed?'

Charles swivelled his head around to check whether anyone was in residence at the web. They weren't.

'So, it is you. Unusual for you to leave your home and go walkabouts?'

The spider listened contritely, so it seemed, unwilling to commit itself to any kind of answer.

'Well, no matter. You're safe now.'

Almost as soon as the words were out of his mouth, Charles stopped short. I felt him to be checking the truth in his cheery statement. Was the spider really safe? Or had he merely rescued him momentarily before they both succumbed to a watery grave?

'I must admit I hadn't believed it was so serious. The whole thing with lifejackets and lifeboats – I thought it was just protocol. Now here we both are sitting in a puddle belonging to the Atlantic Ocean.'

Neither I nor the spider could make a reply to this, so Charles was free to continue with his train of thought.

'So maybe we should head outside and see how the land lies.'

He laughed alone at his rotten joke.

Still holding aloft the creature, which was beginning to stretch out its legs, one at a time, Charles dug out his cigarette case with his other hand.

'First of all, you need a name. I'm going to christen you "George", after His Royal Highness of England.'

The spider stood perfectly still, as if considering this, and then signalled his acceptance with a speedy return to stretching out the legs on the left hand side of his body.

'Second of all, you need a safe carriage. Now, George, this here tin is my most prized possession. Grandfather Joughin gave it to me on my twenty-first birthday. He got it from a man who had fought in the Crimean War, who told him that these little nicks and cuts were caused by Russian bullets during the Charge of the Light Brigade. I don't expect you to know anything about this but if we get out of here alive I'll tell you all about it.'

There were only a couple of cigarettes left and he removed one of these to slide behind his ear. Next he tipped his still dazed eight-legged friend into the tin, promising, 'This is for the best, George.'

The spider was quite possibly relieved to find itself falling into the snug, dry tin after its recent swim.

Charles placed the tin inside his shirt and stood up slowly. Another surprise awaited him. The floor was no longer even; it seemed to slope ever so gently. The baker took a final slug of whiskey, before screwing the cap on and placing it under his pillow.

'With God's grace, you'll be waiting here for me on my return.'

With the immediate business taken care of, he took a firm grip of the upper bunk and pushed himself towards the door.

'Well, George, we're off!'

❦ ❦ ❦

Once more I found myself drifting back into my past. I couldn't help it; the baker's kindness to his half-drowned spider reminded me of the day I found a tiny bird on the ground in front of our house. I called Da to ask him could I keep it and was most surprised when he said no.

'But why not? I've always wanted a pet. Please.'

He wasn't listening to me, however. Instead, he was peering up at the roof, searching for something. I picked up the little creature and held it close to me. Suddenly Da pointed and explained, 'There now, see? That's where he's fallen from.'

Following the direction of his index finger, I saw a small, flimsy-looking nest that looked as if it had been squashed into the edge of the roof. Just at that moment a squawking bird flew quite closely over our heads.

'And that's the little fella's mother. There's one thing you have to remember when it comes to God's creatures, Sammy.

Never, ever get between a mother and her baby.'

The bird perched herself on the nearest lamp-post and continued to squawk at the top of her voice. Da winked at me.

'Aren't we lucky that we can't understand what she's screaming at us? I'm sure she's calling us the most dreadful names.'

It was a little scary when the mother bird dived from her post to swoop past my shoulders. Her baby chirruped twice and, I had to admit, he did look absolutely terrified of me, despite my stroking his skinny, bony head in my friendliest manner.

'Ach, don't be mauling him, son. She mightn't take him back if he stinks of human hands, especially ones as mucky as yours.'

As his mother sped by me again, I held her baby up in the air, 'Go on. Go to your mother. Just flap your wings.'

Da shook his head and said, 'No, he's not ready to fly yet. But isn't he great for surviving such a fall, the poor thing. You'd have thought the shock would kill him outright.'

'Well, if he can't fly back to the nest, I should probably hold on to him then. His mother knows where he is and she can visit him.'

Da laughed. 'Nice try, Sam. Fortunately for mother and child I've got a better idea. I'm going to ask Mr McCracken if

I can borrow his ladder and put the wee mite back where he belongs.'

Mr McCracken ran the corner shop which was just a few minutes away from us, and he used his ladder to reach the more expensive items that he kept up on shelves near the ceiling.

'I'll be back in a tick and I don't want to see him in your hands on my return. Put him down and just make sure he doesn't stray, although he's probably too confused to go for a walk anyway.'

At this stage I had been joined by some of the other children. The bird's mother kept a cold eye on all of us as we stood around her baby, willing it to do something more than simply stand there, the odd, nervous tweet escaping his beak.

'Well now, Nick, looks like we've got ourselves an audience.'

Mr McCracken had not only lent Da his precious ladder but also Nick, his oldest son, who was very tall and very, very spotty.

'Aye, I see that. Now, where is this lost birdie?'

My friends and I parted ways, allowing my father and Nick to walk through us, step carefully over the bird and lean the ladder against the wall of the house. Nick bent down slowly and picked up Beaky. I couldn't resist naming him, just in case I got to keep him in the end.

'His wee heart is racing.'

The mother suddenly screeched by, obviously upset that Beaky had been picked up again. Nick crouched low to make us laugh, 'Oh, missus, I hope you're not aiming to peck my eyes out.'

My father continued on joking with Beaky's mother as he took the baby in his hand and stepped up the ladder, Nick holding it steady for him.

'Now, here he is, safe and sound. Don't be hard on him. He wasn't running away from you and I don't think he was sneaking off for a fag or to see a girlfriend. He just made a mistake and you can plainly see that he's very sorry for causing so much trouble.'

As soon as Da reached the nest, the mother bird landed on the roof, careful to keep her distance as she watched the proceedings.

'Da, Da, what can you see?'

'I see an empty nest, son. No wonder his ma is upset. He's her only chick. There you go, little man, no more high jumps for you. Wait until your wings are stronger. Good luck now and tell your ma I was asking for her.'

We all laughed at this. I really enjoyed the other children laughing at my father's jokes. It made me feel like I was on top of the world. Maybe that's what I missed the most – someone making me feel like I was on top of the world.

❧ ❧ ❧

My plan was to stay with Charles and George for a while, but the baker was walking so slowly, edging himself along the corridors, either because of the sloping or the whiskey and I had so much to do yet. I hurried off, determined to come back and check on him. I wanted to visit the upper deck, once more, and see what was going on. Time was ticking on and I had a hunch that the real work had yet to begin.

Chapter Ten

On my way to the deck, I decided to drop into the first-class lounge. I hadn't been here in a while. In the corner of the lounge was a group of gentlemen thoroughly absorbed in their card game. There were five players in all, dressed impeccably in evening wear, starched-white collars, perfectly creased trousers and shoes that had never trod in anything untoward. Although the men looked calm, they didn't seem cheerful. Indeed, their poker game was a rather sedate one. Cigars were being duly puffed on and the sombre steward continued to serve up drinks as requested.

'Arthur, brandy and ice, please.'

'Right away, sir.'

It could have been an ordinary evening on an ordinary ship. Maybe having lots of money does make you a better person. You mightn't scare that easily if you know you had the money to buy your way out of anything – or almost anything.

Outside, there were plenty of people milling around the deck. I must admit it was hard to believe that such a large, noisy crowd was in mortal danger. The band played on and looked genuinely happy to be performing this important concert, regardless of the fact that they only seemed to be performing to each other. Wallace beamed at his men as he raced his bow over the strings of his violin. I stayed beside them, just for a minute, because the atmosphere among the musicians was as warm and positive as the one among the engineers and Guarantee Group, all these men doing their job of looking after the passengers who – understandably – hardly noticed their efforts. Although I was sure that panic would greet the end of the music and the lights that cheerfully glowed from every window and porthole.

I had to fight the temptation once more to hide away from the ever-pressing fact that *Titanic*'s bow was definitely sinking into the Atlantic Ocean. Harold Bride was standing near Wallace and his men, obviously checking, like me, the state of affairs. The lines on his forehead told me that he also sensed the mood of the crowd.

There was a hint of terror in the air now. Many of the

lifeboats had been rowed off into the night while hundreds and hundreds of people began to grow restless over the few seats left. A loud bang made a few women scream. An officer had fired his gun into the air as a warning to the unruly mob that threatened to rush onto an already crowded boat. Elsewhere some of the male passengers had tried to escape by hiding between the women and children. It was a huge change from the crew's previous difficulty in trying to persuade stubborn passengers to board the lifeboats.

The sounds of a passionate argument reached my ears and I went over for a closer look.

'But he's a child, for God's sake!'

'I'm sorry, sir, but I've got two boys, myself, of thirteen and fourteen years, and he looks plenty older than them.'

The father looked wild with confusion as he pleaded with the stony-faced officer, 'I can't believe this. He's only sixteen. You've got to let him on that lifeboat, I beg you!'

'I'm taking only women and children, as instructed by Captain Smith.'

'But you're saying that this boy is an adult. How can you? Do you see any stubble on his chin? Can't you see the fear in his eyes? I tell you, he's still a child.'

The frightened boy stood behind his father, staring at his feet. I felt him wishing that his father would just accept the officer's decision and walk away. Anything would be better than this embarrassment.

He was lucky to have a father to fight for him.

'How would you feel if someone like you condemned your children to staying onboard a sinking ship? He's my only child. Please!'

Suddenly the heated discussion was over, the father having said the only thing to make the officer change his mind. Scowling at the boy who was the cause of all this trouble, the officer shouted, 'Oh, just get in and be quick about it. We're launching immediately.'

There was no time for a farewell and the boy never got to thank his father who, at least, looked satisfied that he had managed to save his son.

Some of the crew were confused about whether it was women and children *only* or was it women and children *first*, and then the men could take the remaining seats? Captain Smith's name was mentioned, but no one seemed to know where he was. As a result, some were letting men on and others weren't.

A young mother clutching her newborn baby was being encouraged to board one of the last few lifeboats.

'Missus, will you come on? We can't wait for you.'

She was without a chaperone. Perhaps her husband was

waiting for her to join him in America, where he had already found a job and a place to live. She was dressed quite plainly but neatly, suggesting that she was travelling second class. Used to having first her parents take care of her and then her husband, she must have felt very scared and alone, except for the precious bundle in her arms – this tiny, defenceless mite who was hers alone to protect. She had to be both mother and father to it and, therefore, she was unwilling to trust anyone else with her child's life. And this, I realised, was her problem. To climb into the lifeboat, she would have to hand over the baby to someone until she took her seat.

Moving over beside her, it was almost as if I heard her thoughts as clearly as if she was saying them aloud. Her biggest difficulty was the fact that she didn't know anyone else on the ship:

What if I have to take that seat right at the back and there isn't enough time to get Brigid to me before they launch the boat? What if one of those mothers has to hold her until we reach the water? If the boat suddenly lurches – like the others have – they might let Brigid fall, to look after their own flesh and blood. How I can trust any of them with my child? I can't. I just can't.

The officers in charge were much too busy for her to try and explain her misgivings. What on earth was she going to do? Suddenly a male passenger approached her. He was

148

youngish, with an open, honest face, the type you would trust immediately. His large, brown eyes had observed everything. Someone else might just have seen a silly girl who was wasting time needlessly. This well-dressed gentleman, however, saw a young mother in distress and quickly recognised what was making her so.

'If you would allow me, madam? I understand your fear in letting go of your baby. You have my word that if you give me your child and climb into the boat I will pass it to this officer here and instruct him personally to hand over the child to you, and you alone, as soon as you step onboard. Would that be acceptable to you?'

The woman's features filled with an exquisite relief, that, in the midst of all the noise and near chaos, this kindly man understood her plight so well.

Too moved to speak her thanks, she could only nod her acceptance as the tears crept steadily down her face. Together they went up to the officer who, of course, listened carefully to what this first-class passenger was telling him to do. Then, without any further delay, the young woman was helped into the boat where she immediately stood and waited with outstretched arms. The infant, blissfully asleep, was gently passed from the passenger to the officer who had to almost step into the boat himself in order to deliver the precious parcel back to its impatient mother. Not moving away until he saw the woman and her baby safely seated, the man waved his farewell and returned to sit on a nearby deckchair. I felt a rush of love for him. It was such a small act that had heroic consequences. Two lives had been saved for no other reason than he wanted to be of help.

❧ ❧ ❧

I had a hankering to locate Captain Smith. His name was heard throughout the busy deck, yet no one seemed to know where he was. I found him in his quarters, a sorry sight indeed. He was without hope of any kind. The air about his rooms was grey and bleak. There was no pulsating atmosphere here, nor battling heart. Sitting on the side of his bath, he addressed his piteous reflection in the mirror:

'There is nothing more to do. Yet they keep pestering me with questions as if they believe I can change what's happening, but I'm only a man. Help is too far away and there aren't enough lifeboats. What am I to do about that?'

I felt he met my gaze in the mirror. If he could see me, he didn't show any surprise, so I couldn't be sure.

'My last trip ... in every way. No, no, mustn't think like this. It's too soon. How can I have deserved this – after so many years of unblemished service? In less than two hours I will only be known as the captain of the biggest sinking ship in the world. This is to be my legacy. Oh God, it's too much to bear.'

He was so crushed that he couldn't even summon the energy to cry. I felt his pain and his loneliness. No doubt he was right too, about being the one who would be blamed for this – no matter how it ended. But still, he was giving up far too early. He was forgetting that his presence would probably give people some comfort, just like the musicians' tunes and the electricians' burning lights. He had a responsibility to carry on, just like the telegraphists, the officers and the others who were still hard at work.

Is this how you behave? Locking yourself away from your crew and passengers? Ignoring your duties which still exist, and never more so than at a time like this? I am so ashamed of this unworthiness.

It was then I heard another man's voice quite clearly as if there was someone else in the room, but it could merely have been inside the captain's head, I suppose.

Whichever it was, it had an enormous effect on the grey-haired man. He let out a gasp of realisation, 'Dear God! What am I doing?'

That was it. His break was over. Fixing his cap on his head and straightening his tie, he flung aside the feelings of hopelessness that threatened his mind, reminding himself that he was Captain Edward John Smith, a British sea captain and he *still* had a job to do.

As had I.

Leaving the captain behind, I was heading back to the lifeboats, to check up on matters, when I heard a man's voice rising in shock and anger, 'Great God, man. Have some pity and let them through.'

A confused-looking steward was attempting to block the path of some passengers who were obviously not first class. Oh my goodness! It was the young sisters who had boarded at Cork, Kate and Maggie, with their neighbour, James, who was pleading their case, 'I beg you, they're not yet eighteen and won't take up much room in a lifeboat.' The steward was contrite, shrugging his shoulders and offering, he knew, a less than satisfactory explanation, 'It's just that rules are rules: first class go first, then second and then third.'

James opened his mouth to argue, but Maggie placed her arm on his and smiled sadly at the steward, 'Maybe you might just let my sister through, sir. I can wait my turn, but she's my responsibility and my mother would want me to do right by her.'

Before Kate could refuse to go anywhere by herself, the steward shook his head, finally deciding, 'No, no. Come on through. It's best if you stay together. But I'm afraid I just cannot let you by.'

James beamed at the man, in sudden friendship, 'No worries there, mate. I just wanted them looked after.'

The girls hugged their friend quickly while the steward told them to be quick, pointing out exactly where to go for the boats. James called after them, 'I'll catch up with yous in New York.'

All this time I had been rushing around, seeing, watching, observing. There had to be more that I could do. There had to be a reason for my being here. It just didn't make sense if I was on this voyage, only to watch it fall apart in front of me, unable to help in any way. Wasn't that what the bandmaster, Wallace Hartley, meant, when he talked about there being a plan for everyone, something that had to be discovered by each of us?

Watching the baker rescue a tiny, half-dead spider and that first-class passenger helping the young mother with her baby, and now James' victory for the sisters, had sparked something within me. The captain struggled bravely with his hopelessness, as did Jack and Harold who still hadn't found anyone else who could help, yet they stayed in their office, Jack unable to free himself from his headphones and desk. Meanwhile the brief flicker of the lights reminded me of the various battles taking place, to keep *Titanic* alive, down in the engine room. Four faces floated in front of me and I just knew that they were mine to look after: Jim, Isobel, Joseph and Sarah. The sea had already taken one person in my life and that was enough. I had to do something for this little family, for this father who reminded me so much of my own. I just had to be able to help them.

Chapter Eleven

Down in third class people were busy packing and it wasn't too difficult to understand why. First-class passengers could leave behind things like trunks of expensive clothes, least favourite jewellery, shoes and hats. If any of these items needed to be replaced, there was plenty of money to do so. It was a very different matter for the poorer passengers. These brave people, who were leaving their homes to make a new life in America, had brought everything they owned in the world. Goodness only knows how long it would take before they found a job and could afford to buy themselves a new outfit. Therefore, they had to bring their tatty suitcases and worn carpet bags with them.

Isobel sat with baby Sarah in her arms and directed Joseph and his father on how to repack their entire belongings back into their small suitcase. The door was open and the corridor outside was filled with people shuffling along with all their baggage. No one seemed to know exactly what was going on. There was no sign of any crew or staff, not since the midnight call for passengers to make their way up on deck.

Once again I slipped in and out of the different compartments, dismayed at the sights of mothers reluctantly waking their children and taking them out of their warm beds, to begin dressing them slowly. How I wished I could scream at them to hurry up. Here and there, little knots of people chattered excitedly about waking up to find water seeping into their rooms. However, since most of these passengers didn't speak English their important knowledge couldn't be shared around. Therefore, mothers didn't know that there was no time to play 'peek-a-boo' with baby's blanket or comb unruly hair until it was flat.

Sarah leant against her mother's neck and closed her eyes while Jim got the case closed and began to button up Joseph's coat. The baby was wrapped up in the *Titanic* blankets she had slept in. There had only been room in the family suitcase for a small, thin rug that Sarah was very attached to and that wouldn't have been enough to keep her warm. Jim took Joseph's hand and spoke to his family, 'Now, remember, we have to stick together. There is going to be a lot of people around us, so stay as close to me as possible.'

Both wife and son nodded and they all stepped over the

threshold, into the noisy throng. They hadn't gone very far before they found themselves in a long queue that didn't seem to be moving anywhere.

'What's up?' Jim asked the man in front of them.

'We've to wait our turn. First and second class are being taken off and then it's our turn.'

Jim smiled down at Joseph and said, 'Well, that makes sense, doesn't it? They got on before us, so they should get off first.'

His son returned his smile confidently, displaying the gap caused by his missing tooth. It had fallen out the previous evening as he chewed his bread. Unsure about what to do with it, and not wanting to leave it behind because it was one of the very few things that he actually owned, he wrapped it up in a piece of paper and shoved it into his coat pocket. Keeping his hand inside his father's, he patiently waited for whatever everyone was waiting for, feeling perfectly safe.

I knew what that felt like. I remembered how safe I felt when I went walking with my father. Every so often he would give Mother a break from us and take me off for a few hours. Sometimes I wondered were we taking a break from her and her moods, but I never said it aloud. Although, when I was eight or nine, I did ask him why she always seemed angry, but he looked so sad that I quickly changed the subject.

One morning I heard her crying in bed, huge, dreadful sobs that scared me. Da wasn't due back for a couple of hours, so it was just me on my own, listening to her. I knocked quietly on her door and was almost relieved when she didn't hear me. Since it didn't feel right to go off to school, I stayed outside her bedroom, feeling sure I could do nothing else. How I wished she would call out and tell me to do something for her. I didn't knock again, even when the crying stopped. Instead I fell asleep, only waking when Da slammed the front door shut. I ran down to meet him.

'What's this? Why aren't you in school?'

I told him about the crying and he went immediately to her room, not even stopping to take off his coat. When he didn't reappear after a few minutes, I fished out my library book and sat down at the kitchen table, losing myself with Robinson Crusoe on his island.

'You should have gone to school.'

Da glanced over my shoulder to see what I was reading. I shrugged, a little hurt that he didn't understand that I couldn't have left her alone like that. He wouldn't have left her either; I was sure of it. He filled the kettle with water and set it on the stove. Sulking slightly, I kept reading, knowing that he was watching me out of the corner of his eye. He sliced two thick slices of bread, one for him and one for me.

Only when the mug of tea and buttered slice were laid before me, did I permit myself to ask what was wrong with her.

He sat down opposite me, taking the time to milk and sugar his tea. The spoon clipped the sides of his mug as he stirred.

'Well, Sammy, I don't really know what to tell you.'

Dipping the tip of his finger into a smudge of butter on his bread, a habit which never failed to irritate my mother, he looked straight at me.

'Ach, I suppose you are old enough now, and you won't mention it to anyone, will you? Especially your mother.'

I nodded dutifully, though I was beginning not to want to hear what he had to say. He would never lie to me and maybe that was all I needed to know. I liked being a child, not having to know everything about everything. However, it was much too late now. I had asked and he was opening his mouth to give me the answer.

'Mother was crying because she was trying to grow another baby, a little brother or sister for you. Only it went away during the night, when you were asleep.'

Although this was the last thing I expected to hear, it struck me as a suitable explanation for the dreadful sadness I heard in my mother's sobs. I picked up my bread and took a small bite while Da waited for me to say something. My mind was empty. Usually when I didn't know how to explain myself properly he would help me out, but this time he stayed silent. Maybe he didn't know what to say either. Finally I could only think to say, 'I'm sorry she's upset.'

He took a mouthful of his tea and said almost to himself, 'I'm sorry too, Samuel.'

By the time I finished my bread, I had another question but I couldn't bring myself to ask it. Even in my head it sounded very selfish. I wanted to ask was I not enough for her? Instead, I hid my bewilderment behind my book, which I stood in front of my plate, and began to read, the same page over and over again. Da looked so tired that day. Afterwards I wished I had asked him. And I would have, had I known that one day, not too long after that, he wouldn't come home again.

Instead of reaching out to one another, when we lost Da, Ma and I spent the next few years building a wall to protect us from the other. A couple of months after he went, I woke up one night to find her standing beside my bed.

'Ma? Ma? What's wrong?'

She wasn't even looking at me; rather she was looking over my head. The vague look on her face suggested that she was deep in thought. I was just about to call for Da when I suddenly remembered he wasn't there anymore. The shock was far worse than when I first heard he was dead and I started to cry. However, those tears of sorrow soon turned to rage. I was so sick of being sad and scared. She was my mother. Why wasn't she helping me, taking care of me? I sat up straight and was overcome by a need to do something big and loud. I wanted to slap her. I really did. A fire surged through me. It was all so unfair. Why did he have to be the one to die? Why wasn't it her that fell into the sea? Before I knew what I was doing, I was screaming at the top of my voice, 'Get out! Get out of my room!'

For a moment I thought she couldn't hear me. She blinked once or twice and then flung me a look of pity and contempt. 'You're too like him. It hurts me just to look at you.'

The next day we both pretended that the previous night had been nothing but a bad dream.

Sarah and Joseph were very lucky to be loved so much by their mother.

The obedient queue in third class waited and waited. It grew quite stuffy in the corridor and it didn't help that most people were wearing as much of their wardrobes as possible because there wasn't enough room in their suitcases. There was a tension in the air, but not enough to provoke anyone to question their trust that they would be taken care off as soon as it was their turn. As I passed by one woman, she shuddered against her companion, 'Oh! I just felt someone walk across me grave.'

Because I couldn't think of an alternative, I waited with them. Someone would have to come for them, for no other reason than there was so many of them.

'Jim, can you see Kate and Maggie anywhere?'

'No, I can't but sure their Longford neighbours will take care of them.'

At Isobel's sigh, Jim turned to reassure her, 'It can't be much longer now.'

Suddenly there was a cry from farther down the corridor.

'Oh my God! There's water everywhere.'

The effect on the crowd was instant. Waves of fear rolled over the heads of the men, women and children. Sarah was jolted awake when her mother turned quickly to see where the shout had come from and back around again to see if there was any movement ahead. There wasn't, apart from nervous fidgeting and heads swivelling to check on what everyone else was doing.

It only occurred to me then to see what was causing the hold-up and it was simply this: the queue was headed by a timid group who thought nothing of standing patiently, on a sinking ship, in front of a padlocked gate. The gates must have been locked to prevent the steerage passengers from swarming the upper decks before their turn. Slipping through to the other side, I dashed around but could find no one who might help. Indeed, the corridors above were empty. Most people were on deck now. It appeared that the few hundred below had been simply forgotten about.

I hurried back downstairs, wondering what on earth I could do. Why were they all just standing there? Jim was trying to hide the fear in his eyes. He put the suitcase down and lifted Joseph into his arms, who naturally felt his father's anxiety.

'What are we waiting for, Da?

I didn't hear the strained reply because my attention was suddenly grabbed by baby Sarah. It was incredible, but it actually seemed that she was smiling at me, and even waving her chubby arms towards me as if she wanted me to take her from her mother. Could she really see me? Since I was hovering above Isobel there was no one behind me, so it certainly seemed that she could. To test her, I smiled back, a broad, hearty smile and stuck out my tongue, for good measure. To my amazement, and pleasure, she flung her head back and laughed uproariously. What a wonderful thing it is to be able to make someone else laugh like that. I never knew babies could laugh wholeheartedly, like grown-ups. Her mother and father giggled in spite of their predicament.

'Why, baby, who are you talking to?'

They followed the direction of her outstretched arms and saw nothing but the ceiling above them. Isobel kissed her fondly and whispered to Jim, 'Maybe she sees an angel or a spirit guide. I've always heard tell that very young babies can see what others can't.'

Wow! Was this what I was?

This was probably the nearest I had ever been to a baby. I never realised how beautiful and friendly they were. Sarah had decided she liked me without my having to do anything except smile back. Her big, blue eyes were trained on me, eagerly waiting for me to make her laugh again. I put my finger on her nose and she stretched out to do the same to me. Then I held up my finger and moved it quickly to and fro, in front of her face, watching her eyes bounce from side to side in her effort to follow it. Again, she stretched out for me to take her, pouting loudly when her mother, quite naturally, made no move to release her to me.

As Sarah continued to bare her toothless gums – I was fascinated at how she was unable to smile without opening her mouth – I suddenly knew what to do. Or, at least, I knew what Sarah's family had to do. They had to forget about the locked gates and use another way of getting to the lifeboats, like the Firemen's Stairway. This was the narrow, spiral stair-case that had been especially built for the grimy, coal-faced workers: the firemen, the trimmers and the greasers, so that they wouldn't pose a bother to the passengers with their dirt and sweat; that is, the first- and second-class passengers. Things were a little more relaxed for those in steerage. After all, they were the ones living closest to the boiler rooms below. The walkway off this main corridor, to the stairway, was through a plain, discreet door marked 'Staff Only', and it was about twenty giant footsteps away from the family.

I returned to Isobel's side and began a game of 'Clap Hands', whereby I clapped mine over and over again, in the hope that Sarah would imitate me. She did her best and then, when she managed to bang her hands together, she became distracted by her mother who congratulated her on perform-ing such a wonderful trick. Jim hardly noticed any of this. The lights had flickered for just two seconds and also, I was sure, he had detected the slight tilting of the floor. His tense face was a definite reminder that there wasn't much time. Clapping my hands and rewarding Sarah with a big smile, I began to move away from her, praying that she would strug-gle to keep her new playmate in sight. She did. With surpris-ing strength, she flung her whole body against her mother's right shoulder, so that she could watch where I was going. All the while I continued to clap hands and wave them about my head. Unsure if I had a voice, or if she could hear me, I mouthed the words, 'Come on, Sarah, come to me,' as dramatically as possible.

The child practically stood rigid in her mother's arms and looked extremely put out that I was leaving her behind. Again, she stretched her arms out to me as I now danced around, showing her how much fun I was having ... down the corridor. When I ignored her pleading coos to return, she let out a high-pitched shriek of irritation and immediately followed this up by trying to climb over her mother's shoulder. There was just a handful of people standing behind Isobel and all were much too worried to be engaging with an over-excited baby, which Isobel immediately understood on looking around at them. Up to that point, I think she thought that one of them was teasing Sarah.

The baby was crying after me now. Glancing quickly at her husband, Isobel muttered something about being back in a second and took a few steps in my direction, keeping a watchful eye on her daughter. Delighted to be getting her way at long last, Sarah pretended to jump up and down, waving her arms in triumph. I darted up to her at full speed, stuck my tongue out and flew off again, stopping in front of the door to the stairway.

When she had passed the other passengers, the bewildered mother held her baby out in front of her, allowing herself to be led by Sarah's reactions. With every step she took, I waved my arms in wider and wider circles, continuously beckoning Sarah to join me.

'Who is it you see, sweetheart?'

But Sarah couldn't say. She could only gurgle delightedly for a reply. Meanwhile, her father looked around him, only realising then that half his family were heading in the opposite direction.

'Isobel? Where are you going?'

Taking a few steps more, Isobel stood before me, unknowingly. I beamed at Sarah and again she stretched towards me. This time when her mother followed her child's pointed fingers she saw in front of her a small door that pushed open, at her slight touch, to reveal a stairwell.

'Jim! Jim! Come quickly.'

⚜ ⚜ ⚜

If I thought the family was saved, and my work was done, I was mistaken. Something I hadn't considered was this: no one from third class knew their way around the ship. And why should they? Once on board they had to remain in third-class territory. They had their own lounge/general room, their own dining room and their own bathroom. Therefore, the ignorance of Sarah's family and the others who were following them, regarding the geography of *Titanic*, meant that their progress to the lifeboats was slow. There were many corridors that led to nowhere in particular and many doors to be opened, that provided no help at all.

There were more delays when the small group, which had followed Jim's family, began to realise how sparse their rooms were in comparison to the other classes.

'Would you look at this?' A woman stopped suddenly to contemplate properly the second-class library room. 'Ooh, isn't this grand?'

Some of the others crowded in behind her to admire the furniture, especially the massive bookcase at the end of the room. Wait until they saw first class.

Where I could, I beckoned Sarah to keep following me. This worked well in the beginning, though her parents didn't mention to the others that they were merely following the baby's coos. Joseph kept a firm grip on his father's hand. He also kept an anxious eye on the family's suitcase, no doubt thinking about the stolen cutlery for his mother.

The children in the family behind Sarah's grew restless and asked questions that were ignored: 'Where are we going, Mama? Are we in America yet?'

I could only guess at how the minutes were ticking by. No one owned a watch. At one stage we met a large group of girls and boys who looked rather forlorn. They were heading in the direction that we had just come from. Jim eagerly approached them.

'Excuse me, but could you tell us the way to the lifeboats?'

They looked blankly from one to the other, a few of them shrugging their shoulders matter-of-factly.

The father of the other family, a large man with a red face and a dirty suit took offence to this and shouted at them, 'Here now! Just tell us what we want to know. There's no need to be stuck up about it.'

Again the passengers were met with blank stares, apart from one of the boys, a tall, thin youth whose trousers were a little short for him. He opened his mouth and struggled, so it seemed, with his tongue, to squeeze out three small words that meant an awful lot, 'Please. No Eeenglish.'

The red-faced man was relieved to find that he and his new friends weren't the victims of snobbery. 'Well, why didn't you say so? That's alright then.'

As both groups turned to head off in opposite directions, Jim seemed unhappy to let them go.

'Wait! Where are you going? We have to go up on deck. Captain's orders.'

It was no use. Apart from Please/No/English, there wasn't another word to be had between them. The tall boy only smiled politely and nodded his head. Isobel called her husband.

'Come on, Jim. They don't understand. Perhaps they are following their own orders.'

I recognised their uniform immediately. They were the waiting staff from the very posh A La Carte Restaurant in first class. A mixture of French and Italian, they had been brought aboard *Titanic*, to work, by the flamboyant Luigi Gatti. I had heard him, many times, over the last couple of days, boast about his two top-class restaurants in London, Gatti's Adelphi and Gatti's Strand.

'And now, here I am, running the best restaurant onboard the best ship in the world. Not bad for an ignorant country boy, no?'

He also made sure that his *Titanic* customers knew about his love and generosity for his huge, extended family.

'Tell me, do you see my likeness in the waiters and waitresses? Yes? Well, it's no trick of your imagination. I have torn ten of my cousins from their mothers' embraces to come over to England and earn a good living in my name. Luigi Gatti is not one to forget where he came from.'

But where was he now?

170

Actually, I did know where he was. I had seen him up on deck, chatting to some men from first class as they watched the lifeboats being launched. With his top hat and heavy coat, I almost didn't spot him. He would love to hear, I'm sure, that he blended in perfectly with the wealthy business-men around him.

Meanwhile his staff and cousins had obviously been left to fend for themselves. They were in a sort of limbo, being nei-ther passengers nor crew. They didn't work for the White Star Line company, like the plumbers, electricians, stewards, seamen and so on. They worked for Luigi. He paid their wages and so they answered only to him. Because of the lan-guage barrier, they had made no other friends on the ship. Therefore, in Luigi's absence, there was nobody to advise them or even just look out for them. I had a terrible feeling that they didn't entirely understand what was going on and had decided to go down to their quarters to await further instruction. There was nothing I could do for them, but at least they had each other. Whatever happened they wouldn't be alone.

Over the last three years, I had come to the conclusion that loneliness was probably the worst thing in the world. After Da's death, I looked up 'lonely' in the dictionary. The definition read, 'said of a person: sad because they have no companions or friends; solitary and without companionship'. Thanks to the dictionary I could diagnose my condition as if I was a doctor.

Aside from that awful scene in my bedroom, when my mother told me she couldn't bear to see me, there was hardly a sentence spoken in the house for months on end. It is only now that I understand that she was grieving and missing Da so much that there was no room in her head for anything else. At the time I was only thinking about my own feelings and my own grief.

I wasn't allowed to touch any of his stuff. I mean, he didn't have much, but I did want something of his for myself. Watching Luigi check his hat to see it was on straight, taking the time to run his fingers around its rim, reminded me of my father's pride in his own cap, that was nowhere as grand as Luigi's but, I'm quite sure, was just as important to him.

One afternoon when I came home from school, Mother was fast asleep in bed. She didn't seem to sleep at night; I would hear her moving around the house at all hours, so she usually had to lie down in the middle of the day. I only appreciate now that she might have found the nights too quiet, too dark and too empty. Anyway, on this day, I decided to creep into her room to take Da's tatty, old tweed cap. In my earliest memories of him that cap was always perched on his head, no matter the weather. It had worn thin over the years and the last Christmas that we were all together Mother made good her threat to get him a new one. When he opened her gift, he threw back his head and laughed, telling her it was perfect – no, better than perfect. He removed his old one and wore the shiny, new replacement for the rest of the day, not even taking it off for dinner. Mother blushed in pleasure at his obvious delight.

Certainly she wasn't to know that when he brought me out walking after this, he would take his old cap out of his pocket, once we were a mile or so from the house, and put it on, swearing me to secrecy. The new one was then carefully folded and put away until our return journey.

'It's a lovely present alright, but I just prefer this old thing. We've been through a lot together.'

I managed to find it in the mess of the clothes on the floor, even though the curtains were closed and I could hardly see where to put my feet. Back in my room I slipped the cap under my pillow and, that night, I could actually smell him in my dreams. That was the only time I had the cap in my possession. When I got home from school the following day, it was gone. I berated myself for not keeping it with me, but it just didn't feel right to take it out of the house without her permission. So, I didn't.

When I returned to school, after the funeral, I could only cope with books. I felt too exhausted to deal with people. Books made the perfect friends; they didn't shout at me or want to fight me. They didn't need me to behave in a certain way or ask stupid questions. They just let me be myself, whether I felt sad, angry or nothing at all. The boys in my class didn't know what to do with me now that Da was dead. It was like I had grown a third arm or a second head. Most of them refused to meet my gaze but had no problem staring at me in class. A couple of them, the nosey ones, tried to rudely interrogate me about how he died, but I just brushed by them, ignoring them completely. I was surprised at how easy it was and began to ignore just about everyone else, including my teachers and the neighbours who wanted to know where my mother was. In this way I felt I was allowing myself to sleep during the day, just like Ma. But then I woke up, many months later, and found that I was being ignored in turn. I was so quiet, so dull that not even the school bullies could be bothered to taunt me. Just like the dictionary said, I had no friends and no companions.

Chapter Twelve

'I'm scared, Dada, I want to go home.'

Sarah's big brother, Joseph, had tired of the adventure and I didn't blame him.

'Can we just go back to Ireland? Please?'

Both his parents were much too anxious now, to offer him any real comfort. There was a definite slant in the ship's setting and everything, from the pictures on the walls to the chairs, that they passed, here and there, seemed slightly crooked as a result. Isobel muttered to her husband that she was sure she could hear the ocean lapping against the walls. She struggled to control her nervousness. 'Hush, Joseph, we're nearly there.'

The journey to the lifeboats was taking much longer than anyone expected. Sarah had long tired of our game and looked as fed up as her brother. Her father's face was almost grey in colour, his lips practically invisible, so tightly were they pressed together. He kept up a steady pace, appearing unhampered by the heavy suitcase in his left hand and his sulky son who was dragging on his right hand, in a vain attempt to slow his father down.

At one stage his wife asked him quietly should he not know his way about the ship, since he was worked on it at Harland & Wolff.

'Hush, don't let the others hear that. I only know her from the outside; sure we were never let near her after we built her.'

There was a scream from the mother of the family behind them, 'What's that? Can anyone hear that? It's water, isn't it? I can hear water. Oh my God!'

Everyone looked about them uneasily while her red-faced husband barked at her to quiet herself, 'Of course you can hear water. Aren't we in the middle of the blooming ocean?'

'No, No! That's not what I meant. I mean ...' Here, her voice grew loud and shrill as she began to pound her fists on her husband's chest. 'Don't you hear the waves? They're everywhere, all around us.'

One of their children began to cry and the man felt obliged to grab his wife's arms and shake her.

'Get a hold off yourself, woman!'

With that, he slapped her once across the face, silencing her immediately. She stared at him, dazed, as if he had just woken her from a deep sleep and she hadn't the slightest idea where she was. Her three children gathered about her. The husband seized the smallest one and pushed him into her arms.

'Here you go, missus, this will help you focus. It's up to you to keep him safe. Understand?'

She embraced the bewildered toddler tightly and nodded briefly.

Finally the little convoy reached the first-class deck and unintentionally allowed themselves to relax for the first time since leaving their own floor.

'I can hear music!' exclaimed Isobel.

'Me too! Me too!' sang the children, including Joseph.

As I had expected, the vastness of the first-class smoking room cowed them into reverence. Jim actually whistled, 'Phew, I've never seen the likes of it before.'

He put down the suitcase and proceeded to fold and stretch out his arm in quick succession. Joseph gave him a puzzled look, making his father smile absent-mindedly.

'My arm is numb. I can't feel a thing so I'm just getting the old blood flowing again.'

'Well,' boomed the large man cheerfully, 'at least we know we're not the only ones here. For a moment, back there, I was worried that we were all alone.'

Even I was surprised at the huge crowd that thronged around the room. The same pristine group of gentlemen were still at their table, playing cards and drinking their drinks that were still being served to them by the elderly waiter. Here and there, other men were seated, all dressed in their very best. Some sat together in quiet pairs while others were alone, staring into space, some even trying to read. It was a scene of utter calm, nicely complemented by the uplifting music that wafted in from the band outside. For the third-class passengers, however, it was a bit confusing.

'Perhaps there has been some exaggeration,' suggested Isobel, trying to make sense of it all. 'Or maybe they fixed whatever was wrong?'

Joseph's attention was focused on a solitary, empty glass that was sitting squarely in the middle of a nearby table. I think he was considering whether it was small enough to fit in his pocket. Meanwhile the red-faced man, followed by his family, had wandered off in the direction of the bar. Jim called out to him, 'Where are you going?'

'You go on ahead. I just want a wee taste after all that walking, just something to wet the lips. All he can do is say no.'

Jim stared after him, his face bunched up in disgust. Before he could say what he truly thought, however, he was distracted by the family's suitcase that he had placed beside him on the well-polished floor. It slid gently forward, all by itself. Next he heard his son's disappointed 'Oh no!' followed by the sound of breaking glass.

'It fell off the table, Dada.'

He didn't need a third reminder as to why he had led his little family all the way to first class.

'Everyone button up. It's going to be pretty cold outside.'

Joseph was mystified and asked, 'Can we not stay here? This is really nice.'

His father picked up the errant suitcase and shot his wife a look filled with fear that he couldn't allow himself to voice. 'No, son, I'm afraid not. It's time to go.'

The ornate clock on the wall showed that it was a quarter to two.

They made their way outside, becoming part of the massive crowd that continued to thrive, much to my relief. I hadn't quite known what to expect as this stage. The most notable aspect of this vast multitude was that it was mostly made up of men. I was also uncomfortably aware of the gaping absence of other third-class passengers. The majority of them must still be below deck, perhaps still waiting in line for the gates to be unlocked. There wasn't anything I could do for them, however, because apart from the fact that I knew

I couldn't help everyone, I was horrified to discover that there was only one lifeboat left.

Somebody, either a crew member or a passenger and obviously an animal lover, had released the dogs from their kennels below deck. There were maybe ten or more; it was hard to count them as they instantly separated at the sight of so many people, charging around trying to locate their owners. At the sound of their excited barking, people looked up in surprise, having either completely forgotten or else never realising that there were pets onboard *Titanic*. They provided a welcome distraction for the children who had become scared by the tormented faces of the grown-ups around them.

I spotted Second Officer Lightoller, near the last lifeboat, doing something very peculiar, considering the temperature – he was removing his coat and rubbing his sweating forehead.

One of his ship-mates couldn't help giggling, 'Oy, Lights, are you warm?'

He was the only one removing clothes; everyone else was trying to get some warmth into their bones. Winking at his cheeky assistant, Lightoller took the opportunity to look around him, something he hadn't done since he was sent to look after the first lifeboat. Perhaps because there was no time for distractions or any kind of falseness I was finding it much easier, as the minutes ticked by, to hear people's thoughts.

What a sight!

He peered out into the darkness, just about able to make out the ghostly white rowing boats that were ferrying the luckier passengers away into the night. Overhead millions of stars twinkled merrily in the sky.

How can all this be happening on such a perfect night?

Just then he spotted someone he knew.

'Hemmings? What you are doing here? I thought I packed you off ages ago, on Lifeboat 6?'

The man waved at him cheerily. 'Ach, there's plenty of time yet.'

Was there? This opinion seemed to be a common one throughout the staff and crew. The bellboys were over in the corner, smoking away and enjoying the chance to relax, without being bothered by snotty passengers or grumpy supervisors.

Lightoller shook his head in wonder.

Do they think they're on holidays? Then again, what else are they supposed to do? I wish I could bloomin' join them.

First Officer Murdoch was calling out for any more women and children. Jim was ushering the family towards the boat. There was still a trickle of female passengers being sent through the crowds of waiting men who hadn't given up hope of getting a seat on the few boats that were left. Nearby, a young woman stood hand-in-hand with her smiling husband and baby daughter. None of them moved from the spot, despite Murdoch's calls. The wife grinned at Lightoller when he caught her eye.

'Shouldn't you and your little girl be on your way?'

'Not on your life. We're in this together and that's the way we'll go out, if needs be.'

The three of them kept a firm grip on one another and, nodding cheerfully at the officer, moved away, looking for all the world as if they were simply enjoying an evening stroll before bed-time. Lightoller felt a surge of pride in their strength and stood watching them until he was interrupted by a man, another husband and father.

'Excuse me, sir, but I've been told you are letting down another lifeboat.'

Lightoller eyed Jim, as if expecting trouble. 'Well, yes but I'm afraid I can't let you on it. It's women and children only.'

'Yes, I know that, but you'll take my wife and children?'

'How many?'

'Just two, sir, and the baby will sit on her mother's knee.'

'Very well. Bring them over here immediately. I can't hold seats; there are still plenty other passengers.'

Jim grabbed the officer's hand in thanks before calling

back, 'Isobel, this man is going to put you into his boat.'

Gathering his men about him, Lightoller made preparations to set about launching the last boat. He had no time to give this family, only shooting the father a warning look as the stricken wife stood fast, clutching the baby in her arms, at her feet a pale-faced young boy. Turning his back on them, the officer shouted out for any more women and children to come forward.

Hardly believing that this moment had finally arrived, I went back to being an observer once more. Isobel opened her mouth to say goodness knows what while her husband crouched down to talk to his son, 'Joe, you look after Mam and Sarah. I need you to take my place, just for tonight anyway. Alright, lad?'

Joseph looked from one parent to another, slightly unsure of what was being asked of him. However, he knew the right answer to his father's question.

'Yes, Dada. Can you not come with us? The suitcase is too heavy for me to carry.'

'No, son, I can't go yet. You heard the officer: women and children are going first and then the men will follow later. I'll keep the case with me.'

This made sense to the boy. 'Alright, Dada.'

Father kissed son on the cheek and stood up abruptly. His

baby daughter reached for him but, instead of taking her like he usually did, he leant in and tickled her on the nose. Oblivious to her father's tears, Sarah giggled delightedly. She loved when he played with her like this. His wife hardly blinked, not wanting to lose sight of him for even a second. Jim reached into his jacket for his wallet which contained a small amount of money, all the money they had, and handed it to her.

'Here, hide it in Sarah's blankets.'

He looked full into her eyes and moved in close, whispering to her, 'I'll find you if it all works out. If not, go home to your parents. I'll be there, waiting for you. Whatever happens I'll always be with you and the children. I promise.'

With that he hugged her and the baby briefly and fiercely, stopping then to take Joseph's hand and lead them back to the officer. Isobel cried silently as she was helped into the lifeboat. Jim took one precious moment to raise his son to him and inhale his scent and murmured, 'Don't forget me, will you, child?'

Joseph looked horrified at the very idea. 'But you're my da!'

'Of course, I am. Sorry, Joe, I'm just being silly.'

The already lonely husband, and father, stepped back to the suitcase – it was all that he had left of his life and theirs –

and clasped it to his chest, a poor substitute for the warm bodies of his family.

I felt overwhelmed by his sadness and wrenched in two, half of me wanting to remain by Jim's side, while the other half wanting to get as far away as possible from the desolate scene. Joseph was lucky in his ignorance; a child should never have to deal with the likes of this.

Isobel took a seat, a wild look upon her tear-stained face. She wrapped an arm around Joseph, holding on to him and his sister for dear life. Others made their way into the boat after them, frequently blocking the sight of her from her husband who stood at the railings, struggling to hide both his immense sadness and his own fear. But then it occurred to him, as the heads of strangers bobbed up and down, allowing him to see only his wife's shoulder or Joseph's elbow, that he had done a most wonderful thing – he had saved his wife, son and daughter. Hundreds more, he knew, were still below deck, but Isobel, Joseph and Sarah were now being lowered down the side of the ship. This just about made up for the fact that it was his dream of reaching America that had put them into this position in the first place.

This new-found realisation brought an overwhelming sense of gratitude and true happiness. He watched the boat reach the water after a considerably shorter journey than experienced by the earlier lifeboats. In other words, *Titanic* was setting more and more into the sea. Determined to inspire the same feeling of confidence in Isobel, so that it might sustain her through whatever lay ahead, he leant over the side of the wounded ship and roared a hearty farewell, 'See you soon, my dears!' In the darkness, he could just about make out the little arm of his son waving back at him.

Chapter Thirteen

As Jim stood at the railings, watching the distance grow between him and the lifeboat, he was joined by an older white-bearded gentleman. I was sure I had seen him before, either in the first-class dining room or in the lounge. He had caught my attention for the simple fact that he was never without a book in his hand. In fact, I could see one now, bulging out of his coat pocket.

I was so happy to see Isobel and the children launched safely, although I felt the awful wrench at their separation from Jim. Yet, I sensed that I had achieved something, at long last. Surely I could share Jim's pride at getting them off *Titanic*. Emboldened by this, I wanted to take a quick runabout to see if there was anything else I could do, but I didn't want to leave Jim alone. Fortunately I didn't have to worry.

'Would you care to join me for a quick brandy? It would

heat you up. Such a cold night, isn't it?'

Jim's relief at this kind invitation covered his surprise at being addressed by such a well-dressed gentleman. 'Thank you, sir. I don't know anyone here and wasn't sure what I should do.'

'Yes, it's a strange one alright. Let's head inside.'

I went with them, finding myself unwilling to leave Jim just yet. Were I still flesh and blood I could have left with Isobel. I was only fifteen, wasn't I? What I mean is that I was just as scared as any other child; only every other child here had at least one of their parents with them, while Jim, who had always reminded me of Da, was the nearest I had to a mother or father.

As the two men walked together they found themselves, rather suddenly, the centre of much attention. The assorted dogs that had been racing around, in all directions, had re-grouped and surrounded us, barking fiercely and pawing the air.

The old man merely nodded. 'It seems we're not alone.'

Jim wasn't sure if the gentlemen meant the dogs and looked politely confused.

'I mean, I think you might have a companion of some sort, that is, the supernatural sort,' the old man explained with a slight smile.

I was shocked. Could he be talking about me?

The grey-haired gentleman went on watching Jim's face with interest and added, 'You know what I'm talking about, don't you?'

Jim shooed the dogs away, using the threat of his suitcase, lightly whacking the nearest one across the nose. 'I don't know. Maybe. It's just that we were downstairs waiting for the gates to be unlocked. Only no one came back for us. I'd still be standing down there if it wasn't for the baby, Sarah, wanting to go down the corridor, as if she could see someone and wanted to play with them. She led us, if you like, through a door to a staircase we hadn't known about. Anytime I was unsure of what direction to take, Sarah would start reaching towards what turned out to be the right way forward, at every turn. Isobel, my wife, believes in guardian angels and she thought that's what it was. I wasn't sure either way, but ...'

'But you ended up at the lifeboats in the nick of time to send your family off safely.'

Jim chuckled, 'Yes, yes, I suppose so.'

Neither of them could see me, but I was nodding away in agreement and possibly even blushing, though I couldn't be sure.

On entering the first-class luxurious smoking room, the man, who had introduced himself as Mr Stead, chose two leather chairs that were no more than a couple of feet from the bar. The red-faced man and his family were nowhere to be seen, much to Jim's guilty relief. The waiter, on seeing the gentleman, immediately poured two brandies and brought them over with a dignified blow.

'Thank you, Arthur.'

The two men took a first sip in silence. Mr Stead said appreciatively, 'I don't drink much stuff like this because it makes me too sleepy to read. However, on a night like this, it's rather perfect. Wouldn't you agree?'

Jim smiled uneasily. All around him were the unmistakable sounds of a ship in trouble. Things rolled off tables and, every so often, chairs edged forward as soon as you stopped looking at them. There were also the sounds of upset, a sobbing child or a woman appealing for someone to save her. Naturally his thoughts were full of Isobel and the children. He hadn't even thought to ask where the lifeboats were heading.

Now here he was, a poor man all his life, sitting in the most glamorous surroundings he had ever seen. His mind was so muddled that his head hurt. And on top of his confused and distracted state, he had absolutely no idea how his night was going to end.

'Do you think heaven looks like this?'

He surprised himself with his own sudden question. Mr Stead glanced around, trying to imagine how this first-class smoking room might appear to the distracted young man. He answered Jim with one of his own, 'Do you think you're going to die tonight?'

Jim stared back at him and replied slowly, 'I don't know. It's hard to be sure, one way or the other. Isn't it?'

The mad smiled and agreed, 'Yes, it is.'

There was a victorious gasp from Arthur, who had been obliged to dive to the rescue of some dainty-looking glasses that had been about to slide off his counter. Jim found himself slightly cheered by the fact that the dignified waiter had thought it necessary to prevent them from falling. That must mean there was hope yet. Arthur obviously believed there was a future for the glasses and it was more than his job's worth to permit them to be lost.

Mr Stead followed Jim's gaze and, somehow, guessed what he was feeling, 'There's always hope, my boy. It's what makes us human.'

The older man went quiet for a couple of minutes. Jim watched the people around him until the man spoke again. 'Whatever does happen tonight, never forget, young man, that we're all part of history.'

'I'm sorry, sir, I don't think I understand.'

'Well, this is the biggest and most luxurious ship ever to be put out to sea. *Titanic* didn't exist a few short years ago; she was just a man's dream, a fantasy. Today, she's part of the new world, where all sorts of men are making important discoveries and pursuing knowledge just because they're curious. Electricity, motorcars and massive ships are just a few examples of how much the human race has progressed in the last while.

'Perhaps that's one of the reasons some call her the "Ship of Dreams". It's what all her passengers, rich and poor, have in common; we were here first, on the biggest ship in the whole, wide world. Don't you see? You, your pretty wife and children are part of history forevermore – undertaking this epic journey like true adventurers or pioneers. We are the chosen ones, never to be forgotten. She is bound to us as we are to her.'

It was thrilling to hear the man talk like this. That's exactly how I felt, how I had *always* felt, from the moment I presented the first-ever boiling hot rivet to Ed and Charlie to the day I crashed to the ground, and now I believed it even more. We were all part of her, everyone who built her, worked on her and sailed on her. Hadn't Jack scandalised Ed by loudly declaring on the morning of her launch, 'God may have created the world but it was us who created *Titanic*.' In the end, even Jack gave in to sharing the same pride I had always felt.

My dear *Titanic*, damned to transform her very first passengers into her very last, would, in exchange, offer them immortality. Wasn't that what Mr Stead meant?

He took another sip, swirling the brandy around his tongue before swallowing it. 'There is real spirit on this ship. I don't just mean ghosts or even ...' he lifted his glass and winked, 'spirits like this brandy or whatever else Arthur is hiding behind the bar. No, I mean that amongst the passengers, crew and *Titanic* herself, we have shared something very, very special indeed.'

The two men finished their drinks in companionable silence, jumping only slightly when a chair fell on its side. When their glasses were empty, the old gentleman reached into his pocket for his timepiece. Jim couldn't help admiring the elegant watch on its silver chain.

'Well, my boy, it's ten after two o'clock. I'm not too sure about the importance of knowing the time, at a time like this; I am merely giving into a long ingrained habit of mine.'

They were the only passengers left in the lounge. The only other occupant was Arthur, who was scowling as he attempted to squeeze his lifejacket around his coat.

'Do you think we should go out on deck again?'

'Yes, it's probably best. If I could suggest, it might be a lot easier for you to leave your suitcase here. It looks rather heavy and will only get in your way. If I was you, I'd hide it behind the bar. That way, it will be waiting there, safe and sound, for when you need it again.'

Of course, the words '*if* you need it again' were left unsaid, but were plainly heard by both men, nevertheless.

Jim followed the sound advice, stowed away his family's belongings, and the two men made their way outside, back towards the sound of the lively music and the huge crowd.

⚜ ⚜ ⚜

I sensed Captain Smith nearby and found him splashing his way through the corridors. He was making a last trip to the boys in the Marconi-office.

Their door was closed in a useless effort to keep the water out. Nothing much had changed in my absence. Jack was still at the desk, pounding out his frantic messages, while Harold stood by, wishing he could be of more help. The only difference was the green water that was pooling around their ankles. That hadn't been there the last time.

The sight of the telegraphists still working away, despite the Atlantic seeping into every crevice of their tiny office, believing that they might be able to save everyone, made the old man swell up with emotion. He wanted, I felt, to say something momentous, something worthy of the occasion, and, in fact, he did think of something to say. It was a first line, a perfect opening: 'Your parents would be very proud of you both.' Yet, he couldn't bring himself to utter this fine sentence. For one thing, there was no wonderful second line in his head. There was also the troublesome problem about the tenses. Should he use the past tense, 'would have been proud', suggesting that they were goners, thus giving away the fact that he believed that, at this stage, they were all goners? Shouldn't he behave as if there was still hope? Then again, of all the people still aboard the vessel, these two knew just about all there was to know.

Harold cleared his throat, 'Er ... sir?'

Captain Smith snapped out of his daze, to find the two boys staring at him.

Oh dear, how long have I been standing here?

He looked about the office, like a man taking stock of a place he would never see again. His sadness was immense but he fought to keep it in check. Facing Jack and Harold, he gave them a smile of such pride and sorrow that Jack looked down at his messages, not wanting to hear what was coming next.

Reluctantly, Captain Smith delivered his final verdict – the facts, such as they were: 'Men, you have done your full duty. You can do no more. Abandon your cabin. It's every man for himself.'

Expecting them to immediately rush to the door, the captain moved aside to allow their exit. Nothing happened, however, except that Jack went back to tapping on the radio, refusing to meet his captain's eyes, while Harold shrugged as politely as he could, to indicate that he wasn't leaving either.

What boys, thought the old man, *what boys*.

'You look out for yourselves. I release you both.' Then, almost under his breath, he added, 'That's the way of it at this kind of time.' And then he was gone, with me close behind. As far as I could make out, he was planning to spend the rest of the time at the bridge. I left him to it while I hurried to find the baker.

⚜ ⚜ ⚜

I could hear Charles laughing pleasantly and really wasn't all that surprised to find him sitting on a chair, in the pantry of the first-class dining room, sharing a fresh bottle of brandy with the elderly Dr O'Loughlin. They clinked their glasses, delighted to have found, at this hour, such a likeable friend in one another.

'The thing about the Crimean War was that thousands more soldiers died from disease than they did in battle.'

Charles scratched his chin and expressed his surprise, 'Really? I didn't know that. It just goes to show how important your profession is, sir.'

'It's only as important as yours, my friend. After all, one must eat well to prevent illness in the first place.'

'Right you are, Doctor. I won't argue with you there.'

His glass now empty, Charles stood up. 'Well, I suppose we should head for the upper deck.'

He was only mildly surprised when his companion, instead of moving to follow him, shook his head, his pale blue eyes twinkling all the while.

'No thank you, Mr Joughin. I am seventy-seven years old and have had a satisfactory life, all told. Therefore, I won't be joining you on your further adventures. I think, instead, I should like nothing more than to stay where I am and take a second drink, and then a third and then a fourth, if God grants me the time.'

Much to the old man's relief, Charles didn't try to change his mind. Instead, he offered his hand in acceptance of a decision well-made, and tapped the bottle a brief farewell. 'Goodbye, Doctor. I treasured these brief minutes in your company. God bless you.'

The elderly man, already pouring his second drink, made a heart-felt reply: 'Thank you, dear Mr Joughin. You have been nothing but kindness itself.'

My mind was reeling as Charles strolled through the water-logged corridor. All these scenes of farewell were threatening to overwhelm me. Was this what life was all about? I didn't get to say it to anyone, that day I fell. None of us got to utter it to one another, Ma, Da or me. I felt robbed, cheated out of everything that should have been rightfully mine. What had happened to my family?

Charles was quite drunk but seemed as calm and collected as ever, even as he filled the silence with small talk. Once again I pretended he was talking to me. I imagined us to be walking together, in full conversation, as if we had known each other for years. It helped to take my mind off my own confusing thoughts.

'I never saw this coming, that's for sure. This was the very deck I explored, that day, before any passenger came on board. All this beautiful work, too beautiful to last.'

Suddenly there was the sound of frantic shouting outside. Peering together through the windows of the promenade, we were equally shocked to see people already in the water.

'Surely it's too soon for that to be necessary?' Charles wondered aloud to himself.

We could just about make out heads and flailing arms, the sight of which made the baker shiver. He only noticed now that the ship was sagging in a field of icebergs.

'Why, it must be freezing down there.'

There was a pitiful howl of 'Help, Help, I can't swim,' that made the baker gasp. He had to do something, but what? Waving at the half-submerged passengers he shouted out the rather useless, 'Hang on!' and looked around for something, anything, he could make use of.

Deckchairs were stacked throughout, ready to be dotted around the deck the following morning. Dashing over, he grabbed three at a go and began pushing them through the small windows which wasn't easy. He worked fast, only stopping when there were no more to throw. Meanwhile the shouts from below in the freezing water had stopped.

It was a sobering experience. Charles shivered slightly and sighed. 'So, this is it, then. Well, we'll see about that. Hey, George?'

Setting his shoulders back, his stride became deliberate as he continued on his way.

Chapter Fourteen

'Jack, watch out!'

I heard the sounds of a struggle coming from the Marconi-office and got there just in time to find a man, whose sooty skin identified him as a greaser, trying to take Jack's lifejacket.

Grateful to have a reason to release his pent-up anxiety, Harold roared, 'Hey! Put that back, you thieving bastard! Jack! Jack!'

For the first time since the crash, Jack turned his back on the machine and the two telegraphists tackled the man, grabbing the jacket from him and knocking him down. It was Jack who swung the fist that caught the thief squarely in the mouth. The greaser swooned under the impact and hit the water with a splash. The boys looked at one another, breathing heavily from the unexpected exertion. I don't think either of them had ever been in a fight before.

Jack grabbed a pencil and paper. 'Right, get his name, so I can report him.'

I was aghast. Surely they knew there wasn't any time for this.

Harold shook the unconscious man and asked breathlessly, 'You don't think we've killed him, do you?'

'Don't be daft. Look at his chest; he's still breathing.'

He wasn't dead, I knew that much, but he was definitely out for the count. Even the lapping of the water around his ears didn't wake him up. Harold bent down to try to lift him, but then the lights flickered for maybe two long seconds. Power was on the way out. So, instead, he thrust the precious lifejacket into his friend's arms.

'Please put this on right now. I mean it!'

Jack was finally obedient. Then, just as they gathered themselves to make a final decision regarding their sleeping visitor, they heard the sea. How peculiar that the sight of it in their office didn't hold quite the same terror as hearing it. Jack snapped to attention, eager for action after being trapped in his chair for so long. 'It must be on the bridge. Come on, let's clear out.'

Harold nodded and stepped over the figure on the floor, saying, 'He's probably better sleeping through it.'

Therefore, they left the injured man behind because there

was no time to lose – absolutely no time at all.

❖ ❖ ❖

There was one more person I wanted to find before I went back outside. I made my way back to the first-class smoking room and found Arthur looking for something behind the bar.

'Aha! There you are. Thank goodness for that.'

It was his wallet. How ironic that his wages should be the last thing he would think off, unlike the rich women in first class who summoned their jewels before doing anything else.

As he shoved the wallet into his pocket, he was surprised to find he wasn't alone. There was a lone figure in front of the great fireplace. Arthur's surprise was even greater when he saw it was Mr Thomas Andrews, the very man I was looking for.

There was something very final about the way he was standing perfectly still and staring blindly at the painting over the mantlepiece. His lifejacket was sitting uselessly on a table beside him. Arthur recognised the stance of a man who had made up his mind to do nothing more. The waiter knew it was probably pointless to ask, maybe even rude to interrupt a man's thoughts at a time like this but, on the other hand, he couldn't just walk away from him. So, he cleared his throat politely and in vain, since Mr Andrews seemed completely unaware that he wasn't alone. It was as if he was in a trance. Arthur was, thus, obliged to call out to him in his most respectful tone, 'Mr Andrews? Sir? Aren't you even going to try?'

The ship's designer merely waved one limp hand at the older man without taking his eyes off the painting. Arthur, who was very fond of Mr Andrews, always finding him to be polite and extremely pleasant to serve, raised his own hand in turn and saluted the engineer, adding a hearty, 'Good luck, sir,' before walking outside without a backward glance.

About a second after Arthur left the room, Mr Andrews looked around. Had someone been there or had he just imagined it? It was 2.15am, barely enough time to think about everything. The lights flickered a couple of times, reminding him of the engine room and all the fellows who had cheerfully refused to leave their post.

I have killed them all. I designed her and her flaws and all I have to offer, by way of penance, is myself.

Of course there were many more than Mr Andrews involved in the creation of *Titanic*, but he was prepared to accept the entire blame because that was the type of man he was. Perhaps he even felt responsible for the very existence of icebergs in that part of the world, especially at this time of the year. Arthur couldn't have known all this. He couldn't have understood that Mr Andrews would not be making a go of it while brave men, like his team of engineers and even the little orchestra, had chosen to stay put.

His thoughts filled the room, rebounding off the panelled walls, the chandeliers and the very glasses that Jim and Mr Stead had used.

I am not brave, I have no choice. How could I arrive home, knowing that so many had to stay behind because of a hole opened up by ice, in a ship that I designed? God help me, but my life seems a pitiful penance for such a wanton mess of this scale.

He allowed no room in his broken heart for his beloved wife and baby daughter. That must be the genuine part of his sacrifice, preventing himself from ever seeing them again. They would be alright for money which was more than could be said for the families of *Titanic*'s crew. There now, he would make himself responsible for the hundreds of relatives, bereft of their breadwinner.

Why had this to happen? Had it been wrong of him and his colleagues to attempt such an incredible thing, a ship that was indestructible, no matter what Mother Nature threw at her? Did they make God angry by trying to imitate his perfection? A story he had learned as a schoolboy came floating back to him. It was a famous story from Ancient Greece about a man who made himself and his son a pair of waxen wings, so that they could escape their captivity. The wings work beautifully; the two of them fly off, free at last, exhilarated by the fact that they are soaring like birds. Icarus, for that is the man's name, pushes himself to climb higher and higher and starts to believe that he might actually be able to meet with the gods in the Heavens. His pride leads him to make a fatal error when his outrageous ambition makes him fly too near the sun. Not too surprisingly, the wax wings melt and he falls to his death, with the gods' blessing. The moral of the story is that no mere mortal should ever think he's on an equal setting with the gods.

But surely God wants us to make use of the gifts he has given us. After all, if it weren't for boats, we would never get to see and appreciate the rest of the earth. Boats give us freedom and surely God means us to experience that. The world is a fine, big planet. How dreadful it would be to waste it and remain in ignorance about other countries and peoples across the water.

I went to his side, wishing that I could comfort him. But even if he could have heard me, I was only a boy. His grief was much too big for me.

The painting over the fireplace was a rather cheerful one. It was no wonder that he preferred to dwell on it instead of going outside into the bitterly cold. Norman Wilkinson was the painter's name and his picture was entitled 'Plymouth Harbour'. He must love boats as much as Mr Andrews because there were no less than ten of them, if not more, in his splendid painting. They were all different sizes though none nearly as big as *Titanic*.

There was a wonderful flow to the scene; everything seemed in perfect harmony with everything else. It was all as it should be: blue sky, pretty blue sea, green grass, boats in ship-shape, not a tear from an iceberg in sight, and fishermen relaxing in the morning sun – the complete opposite of what was happening right now. Nothing bad would ever happen to anyone in the picture. The same couldn't be said for those still on *Titanic*.

As I stared at the picture, it went blurry and was replaced by a completely different one. I was looking at Mr Andrews, sitting in a carriage, talking with his wife. He must be remembering it. They seemed to be coming home from a party. She was all dressed up but looked sleepy as she leant her head against his arm.

'And what did you men talk about after dinner?'

'You wouldn't believe it if I told you.'

'Oh, Thomas, now you must tell me. You can't leave me wondering. I won't sleep.'

Mr Andrews laughed and patted his wife on the head. 'All

right, but you're to promise not to be frightened by it.'

His wife moved away from him and exclaimed, 'My dear, you're frightening me now. How can I promise something about which I know nothing?'

'Don't be alarmed, Helen. It's just that some fellow told us that an American businessman, whose name I've forgotten, has cancelled his ticket for *Titanic* because he dreamt he saw the ship disappear into the sea. It's the strangest thing I've ever heard.'

His wife shivered suddenly. 'Oh my, that is peculiar. Maybe you should stay at home, just this once, and get someone else to go in your place?'

'Now, Helen, why on earth would you be worried? Do you not trust your husband?'

His wife was rattled by his reaction. 'Of course I trust you! What a thing to say. And what has my trusting you got to do with anything?'

'Well, if you trust me and my abilities as a designer, then you must know that there is nothing to worry about. You've seen her in the shipyard; you've remarked on her size and apparent strength. So, how could you possibly think that anything could happen to me? She is the finest work I've ever done.'

Slightly irritated by her husband talking about *Titanic* as if *she* were a far superior woman to the one he was married to, Mrs Andrews, nevertheless, was contrite and apologised for her words. 'Oh dear, I see what you mean. I'm sorry, Thomas. Of course you are right. She, *Titanic*, is as splendid as her designer.'

They kissed and made up on the spot.

The laughing couple disappeared, leaving behind the dull reflection of the strained face of Mr Andrews as he gazed upon Mr Wilkinson's clear, blue water. He wouldn't even permit himself the comfort of sitting down to wait. No, he didn't deserve that much. It was only proper and decent that he remained on his feet to face what was coming.

For just a second, just before I took my leave off him, he saw me too, in the painting. I was sure of it. In response to whatever he glanced in my expression, he whispered three words, 'I'm so sorry.'

I shook my head, but it was too late: he closed his eyes in shame, and I had to go.

Chapter Fifteen

How much time was left? I went outside where I was relieved to find the band still playing together. Plenty of people hovered near them without realising it. I felt that if someone had suddenly landed in their midst – like me – and asked them if they were enjoying the music, the accidental listeners might have looked bewildered as they responded, 'What music?'

Wallace had never heard his grandfather's violin sing so sweetly. It was as if the wise, old instrument understood that this was its final performance. He was determined to keep a firm hold of it, no matter what happened. It would take a lot more than water to separate him from such a faithful friend. When he saw the sea begin to swirl its way around the deck, sneaking in and around the wooden legs of the deckchairs, he knew it was time. He took the opportunity to say a few words:

'My dear friends, it has been my privilege to work with

you. I wish to thank you all for your talent, your friendship and your constant support and co-operation with this impromptu concert of ours. Now, with your approval, I'd like to suggest an appropriate melody, one that had been a favourite of mine since childhood.'

They all smiled in ready agreement, content to play whatever he asked of them. Not one thought of walking away. Music would save them, or, at least, the most important part of them. Such was their trust in Wallace that each one of them preferred to stand next to him – as the sound of the sea grew louder – than on any other part of the ship. Wallace positioned his violin into the curve of his neck and strummed the opening notes of that exquisite hymn, 'Nearer My God to Thee'. Theodore, missing his piano, sang out the words:

There let the way appear steps unto Heaven

All that thou sendest me, in mercy given;

Angels to beckon me,

Nearer my God to Thee

Nearer my God to Thee, Nearer to Thee.

He knew how much Wallace loved this hymn, because the bandmaster had told him that this was the hymn he wanted played at his funeral. He sang it now with pride, glad he could do this for his friend. The hymn had also been a favourite of my mother's. I hoped someone had sung it at her funeral.

One family was definitely listening to the orchestra. They swayed almost, keeping time with the violinist, allowing the music to wash away their fears and their not too serious sins. From Sweden, mother, father and their five children, they were preparing to follow through on a decision made earlier. I understood what they planned to do and moved over to be with them. Before Wallace led the band into the next verse, the family formed a close circle, shutting out all other distractions as they held and kissed one another goodbye. Few people took any notice of them as most were caught up in their own looming dilemma. When they felt ready, the parents and children walked to the front of the ship, whereupon they formed a chain by holding hands and then they walked together, side by side, into the ocean. I watched them drown, envying them their absolute love for one another.

The brave Swedes weren't the only ones to take to the water while *Titanic* still lingered. As she nosed down, inch by inch, people who were trapped in the lower decks, with no time to reach the crowd above, found themselves washed overboard or simply took the plunge because, really, that seemed to be their only option.

In another corner a priest prayed with a group of

passengers. His listeners seemed to take strength from his steady voice, 'Our Father Who art in Heaven ...' Those who didn't care for the priest formed their own groups, to say their particular brand of prayers.

Water lapped freely over the front of the ship. This terrifying sight divided the crowd of passengers and crew. The question was whether to stay at the front or else try to leave the water behind by charging to the stern, the back of the ship. Accordingly, some stayed where they were while others began to edge back, reluctantly, all still hoping that this wasn't the end.

I wasn't a prophet, so I hoped, too, that complete disaster would be averted.

All things considered, the atmosphere on deck was calm and reflective. Here and there men shook hands with one another, making promises to contact, if they lived, the relatives of their companions should they not.

'Won't you please take down my mother's address and I'll take yours? We can use the back of my business card. Do you have a pencil?'

The lights still glowed in the windows that were above water and, thanks to this, there was still some belief that all was not lost. Yet, here the water began, with determination, to flood the deck, sending the crowd, in their hundreds, to jog towards the stern. In and amongst the passengers were the staff and crew. I think that they were the most shocked of all; such was their belief that 'their' *Titanic* was unsinkable. Oh, Charlie, Ed, Jack: I'm glad you aren't here to see this.

Meanwhile the band maintained their position between the first and second funnel, continuing to serenade all who were left. I spied Captain Smith all alone in the bridge, twisting and turning the wheel absent-mindedly. He had a clear view of the bow of his ship kneeling further and further into the cold sea.

Second Officer Lightoller and his remaining men were still pulling on the ropes, in a desperate bid to release the last Collapsible boat, the canvas inferior of the hardy lifeboat. The two telegraphists made their way over to him, to see if they could be of any help.

I watched Charles Joughin, Chief Baker, pat the pocket that contained his cigarette case. Deep in thought, he turned his back on the approaching water, to survey the scene in front of him. It was a bit of climb now to the back of the ship where he could see the crowd packed together. I could hear him wondering whether to join them or not. He decided against it because it seemed like a pointless exercise. The alcohol in his blood wouldn't allow him to entertain any silly ideas. It was better to face the inevitable instead of putting it off for just a few minutes more. Therefore, he slowly faced the ocean; indeed, he was already standing in it.

'Well, George, I guess we should be brave and put our trust in the Heavens above that it all works out. What do you think, lad?'

Without waiting for a reply, he blessed himself, waved at the musicians, who were starting to falter, and walked unsteadily to the front of *Titanic* and then off into the sea, in search of one of those deckchairs he had had the good sense to heave overboard.

❧ ❧ ❧

I watched one woman tell her children, two boys and a girl, to wait for her as she crossed over to an officer and tapped him meekly on the arm.

'Excuse me, sir. My husband isn't here and I wanted to ask a man what would be best.'

The officer followed her gesture to her anxious children. 'What do you mean?'

She took a moment to find the right words. 'I need to know what to tell them.'

A father himself, the officer guessed her dilemma. 'You are asking me if you should tell them that they might be about to die?'

She nodded tearfully. 'Or should I say nothing? Give no warning? I don't know what to do. The girl is only seven and the boys aren't much older.'

The officer looked past her to the anxious faces of the sons and daughter.

'I'm sorry, madam. I don't know. I'm trying to picture my little kiddies standing over there but I can't imagine what I'd do.'

Crushed by his response, the mother bowed her head and turned away to rejoin her children.

'Wait a minute.'

The officer couldn't let her just walk away.

'Would you like if I stayed with you and the children? No matter what happens? I'll do my best for you all. I mean, I can only promise you what I'd promise my own family at a time like this.'

For an answer, she hugged him quickly and they walked back to the children together, to talk about great big ships and great big icebergs.

⚜ ⚜ ⚜

Captain Smith readied himself for the violence that he knew was coming. As the ship began to topple, the water crashed through the window of the bridge room. Just seconds before he was met by the ocean, he straightened his collar, puffing out his broad chest, and stood to attention.

Unimpressed by the stripes on his jacket, the ocean knocked him clean off his feet and dragged him back out through the window to spit him into the wide, open sea.

The destruction had begun, at last.

Wallace Hartley and his musicians were finally silenced when a large wave, that was completely unexpected, rolled over the whole length of the ship, thanks to the sudden push downwards of *Titanic*'s bow. The little orchestra were brutally dispersed in all directions. None of them was wearing a lifejacket; there had simply been no time. As Wallace was swallowed whole by the water, he thought, for just a moment, he was being stabbed by a thousand knives, such was the ferocity of the icy temperature. The only good thing about this was that he had no idea he had let go of his grandfather's violin. In his mind, he was still playing his favourite hymn as his eyes closed and his fingers began to freeze. It was shocking how fast they died.

I understood now that I would see everything and that I was powerless to stop it.

It had started with a spurt of green water, just a long, thin, persistent spurt that represented the strength and the sheer determination of Mother Nature, to thread *Titanic* as if she were a great big darning needle. The Atlantic Ocean pushed its way beneath closed doors and over the too-short walls of the water-tight compartments. It trickled up stairways and poured over furniture, the most beautiful, lavish furniture that had ever been sent out to sea. Not content with polished tables, sparkling crystal glasses and dainty chairs, it poured over those men who, knowing no better, had chosen to stay put in order to rescue letters, coal, tools and one another.

The ocean saw no difference between a dinner plate and the elderly man who sat alone in the pantry, sipping quietly from a bottle of cook's brandy. Both were smashed up against the wall without any discrimination. The hard-working staff of Monsieur Gatti, including his ten cousins, heard the roar of the tonnes of water long before it burst through the door: upon them, over them and then rushed on, uprooting beds, wardrobes and potted plants by their thousands.

Mr Andrews, *Titanic*'s popular designer, was flung into the cheerful picture above the mantlepiece. There was nothing personal in this; it was all perfectly natural. The brave postmen missed out on the destruction and, perhaps, that is exactly what they would have wanted. Nothing could stop the water; it ran freely, seeking out every crevice, every nook, every cubby-hole and every passenger who had chosen to wait it out in their cabin.

Those marvellous engineers, the boys and the men of the Guarantee Group, fought to the bitter end. And it was a majestic battle, much like the ones fought by the fearless warriors of Ancient Greeks against the marauding, barbaric Persians, with the engineers pitching themselves against the Atlantic, in the fight to maintain electrical power. Fuses blew out all over the engine room; wires sizzled as the Atlantic proved far superior in strength, deck by deck. Still, they fought on for the remaining passengers and crew. Keeping the lights on was a matter of life and death for those thirty-four battle-worn heroes. When the lights began to go out, window by window, it meant the end of those brave, exhausted soldiers who were finally overcome.

Meanwhile Second Officer Charles Lightoller prayed as hard as he could. He watched in horror as that devastating wave slapped up everything in sight. Screaming at his men to grab something to hold on to, he clung to the side of the Collapsible that stubbornly refused to budge. The two telegraphists were caught off balance and I only saw Harold put up a fight. Had he not caught hold of the corner of the roof over the officers' quarters, he would surely have been lost, just like his friend and colleague, Jack Phillips.

Who knows, maybe Jack had never planned to return safely to his family and friends, back home in England. His guilt over that last ice-warning had overwhelmed him when he finally had to face the aftermath of the collision. It was the same overwhelming guilt that I saw in Thomas Andrews, Captain Smith and Frederick Fleet, who, at least, was safe. Over the previous two hours, Jack had worked in a sort of rage, determined to find help in time. His office, his desk, his chair and, of course, his radio had served as a cocoon, shielding him from what was happening outside.

When he knocked out that poor unfortunate who had tried to steal his lifejacket, he could no longer ignore the noise of calamity and the sea water which chilled his toes. But, when he followed Harold outside, he wasn't prepared for what he would see. There were too many people to even begin to guess at their number. Tears welled up when he spotted individuals in the crowd, a girl of maybe fourteen years, a seven-year-old boy, stranded toddlers and little babies swaddled in blankets. Just before that wave hit, Jack spotted two babies lying on the ground beside one another, having been left to their fate. Their mothers, most likely, didn't want to watch them die. The wave took them in one gulp.

Harold didn't hear his friend's cry of anguish.

'No! No! How can this be?'

Jack did his best to hold on to the Collapsible, but the water was far too aggressive and much too strong for a man who was exhausted and broken. He had fought and fought, never giving in to the belief that all was lost, that nobody was near enough to help. The ocean was greedily consuming the ship's heroes one by one. Officer Lightoller and I were the only ones who saw Jack go under and neither of us could tell Harold that he was wasting his precious breath, calling out for his brave friend.

Dear God, I don't want to die. Make this boat come free, it's our only hope.

I heard Officer Lightoller's prayer as if he had screamed it at the top of his voice. He needed a miracle; just a small one and he would do the rest. And it seemed that his prayer was heard because that same wave that sent so many spilling into the water to a certain death, also wrenched the little boat free, at long last. That was the good news. The bad news was that the force of the wave tipped the boat upside down as it floated off *Titanic*. Lightoller, an immensely practical man, who never looked for perfection from anyone, including God, saw only that his prayer had been answered as best as it could be under the atrocious circumstances. The sea, having reached the roof he was now standing on, allowed him to do just as the baker had done.

Bellowing at Harold, who was frantically looking for Jack, and a handful of officers, he stepped into the ocean after the upside-down boat.

'YOU LOT, FOLLOW ME!'

That large, sudden wave signalled the beginning of the

end. Plenty were washed overboard as if they were being rinsed out of a cup. Men roared and women screamed, only the children were quiet as they concentrated all their efforts in keeping as near as possible to their parents. I felt so helpless.

Oh, my God, Jim. Where was he?

I could do nothing to save my own father but I was damned if I was going to let Sarah and Joseph lose theirs.

There he was, clinging onto the railings, squashed in by the large number of people who were determined not to end up in the water.

The wave unleashed a new, hideous reality as the back of the ship began to slowly stand up out of the sea. Dodging water was one thing. It was frightening, but at least it was straightforward. Standing on the backside of an ocean liner and feeling it rise towards the sky was something else entirely.

Those who hadn't been able to get near to a railing ended up on their bellies, skidding at ferocious speed from that preposterous height all the way down to the water below. Jim managed to hold on, but just about all of the women and children were lost at this point. The kindly officer who had offered to stay by the fatherless young family was nowhere to be seen, like his charges. In other words, he had kept his word to them, to stay with them whatever happened.

The whole world, it seemed, was filled with screams, from the tip of the now vertical *Titanic* to those hundreds flapping about in the freezing water. They seemed so far away from where I hovered next to Jim. He was surrounded by men and they all looked at one another in bewilderment. Were they really standing on *Titanic*'s back, as she herself stood up in the air? How could this be happening? One man, the red-faced man who had led his family to first class, only to stop for a drink, at his family's expense, even tried to make a joke.

'At least it's not raining.'

No one laughed. I looked around for his wife and children, but they must have been in the water. They had missed the last lifeboat because of him and were now drowning if they weren't already dead. I was the only one who saw his tears. His face was distorted with his own torment, but I found it hard to feel sorry for him. He should have been with his family now, wherever they were. Suddenly, as if he heard me, he let go and fell to his death. Nobody said a word.

A few of the men, wracked by fear, forced themselves to stop staring down at the sea and, instead, lifted their gaze to the stars in the sky, the most ordinary sight around. Shooting stars leapt across the sky and all was pretty much as it should be. When nothing happened, after a few seconds, another man spoke up.

'Don't forget to let go just as you hit the water or you'll end up getting sucked down with her.'

No one thanked him, but all intended to heed his words. Then, at last, there was movement. I expected a sudden, aggressive rush downwards, but it was the opposite. I felt the stricken ship was trying to accommodate her remaining passengers who had fought to stay aboard her until the very last minute. She very gently slid down, making a slow, elegant descent. The shouting was immense, however, and I lost sight of Jim after he hit the water. I hovered over the exact spot, hoping and hoping that he wasn't still wrapped around the railings. When he finally emerged, spluttering, coughing and spitting out the salty water, I could have cried, if I had been able to.

As *Titanic* slid below the water, I found myself unable to follow her. I kept her in sight for as long as I could and then she was gone. I could hear her bell chiming and I remembered Charlie saying, back in the shipyard, that the sound of the rivets being struck by the hammers probably sounded like church bells on the wind. She was wrenched in two, at least that's how it looked to me, the Atlantic finishing her off for good. Such cruelty. She didn't deserve this; none of us did. A couple of minutes, or perhaps it was seconds, passed before I heard her dash into the seabed. It was so confusing. I had thought that I was to remain her passenger for as long as she lived, that she was my grave which was a lot more interesting than a box in Belfast City Cemetery. But no, just like me she didn't get to live long enough, thanks to a stupid accident at work. None of it made sense. What had it all been for – all those workmen, all those months of building her? Now, here we were, both lost at sea. We had shared the same fate. Perhaps that's why I had always felt so close to her.

I couldn't even begin to guess how cold the water was. Every time Jim breathed out, a cloud of mist – his own – almost obscured his face. Then the dying started in earnest. Whether it was the shock of the freezing temperature or the shock of such a traumatic experience, people seemed to fall asleep after a few short seconds. I spotted Arthur, the old waiter, lying perfectly still, his lifejacket keeping his body afloat. Jim was shivering so violently, it was like he was having some sort of fit. I became afraid for him all over again. What was I going to do now?

There was a shout from behind me and I saw, with amazement, Officer Lightoller and Harold scramble on to the back of an upturned boat. Taking a minute to look about, I could also see most of the other lifeboats in the distance. Were Isobel and the children nearby? All around me people were sobbing for help. Surely some of the boats would come back to pick them up? The chorus of echoing voices reminded me of Da taking me to see a football match in Windsor Park. Minutes were ticking away and the shouts grew less and less. Jim was still alive. I could see his foggy breath, but oh, how I wished he would shout out like the others.

Lightoller and Harold had been joined by a rather straggly bunch of men, all standing one behind the other, balancing on the spine of the boat. I was overjoyed to see the baker swim by me, making for the boat. He took his time with wide, even strokes, as if he hadn't a care in the world.

'I say, lads, any room for one more?'

Lightoller shook his head sadly, 'I'm sorry, mate, but we can't take on anyone else or she'll tip over.'

Mr Joughin just nodded his head agreeably, 'Yes, I see. Not to worry. I'll go and catch up with one of the lifeboats.'

Without waiting for an answer, he swam around the back of the boat. Suddenly one of the men at the back of the line whispered, 'Charlie? Is that you, mate?'

Before the baker could identify himself, his colleague had reached out a hand to him and, helped by a second accomplice, pulled him onboard. Lightoller was too distracted with giving directions to the others regarding steering the boat using the weight of their legs. I heard the baker's whisper, 'Now, George, hang on there. We might just make it yet.'

Their progress was dreadfully slow. Unfortunately Jim was

silent as they passed him so they kept going and he was left behind. Though, perhaps, Officer Lightoller wouldn't have allowed him onboard in any case. The cloud of breath was growing fainter and smaller and his face seemed to be taking on a bluish colour. If only I could scream or punch him to stay awake. Why was he just giving in like this? Had he forgotten about Isobel, Joseph and Sarah? Didn't he realise he had to fight?

There was a small splash a few feet away from me. It was one of the dogs and it was struggling to keep itself afloat. Maybe it understood that if it kept kicking out, it might help to stave off the stinging cold. Then I heard another splash. Turning away from the dog, I saw a marvellous sight, one lone lifeboat was returning to the rescue. The officer at the helm was swinging his torch left and right, while calling out, 'Hullo? Hullo? Is anyone there?'

There were two other men in the boat prodding the bodies they passed with their oars, to see if they were still alive. One of them was visibly upset as each body rolled over lifelessly.

'We waited too long. May God forgive us all! Most of 'em were probably dead as soon as they hit the water.'

His superior refused to accept this and re-doubled his efforts. 'Come on! There must be somebody here? Make yourselves known.'

Jim's breathing was getting slower with each passing second. There was no time to lose. The would-be rescuers were about fifteen feet away from him. I couldn't afford to wait until they browsed around, in the hope that they might see the bit of life left in him. As it was, they hadn't noticed the clumsy paddling of the dog. It was still dark, after all. Suddenly I knew what I could do. I launched myself at the dog, hoping that he wasn't too caught up with his own battle to survive, to notice my 'woo-hooing' like a proper ghost. I couldn't actually hear myself, but I kept repeating it over and over again as I hovered right next to the animal's face. To my relief, he stopped what he was doing, looking about him puzzled. Then he let out a meek yelp. It was the most beautiful sound I had ever heard.

'Go on, boy. Bark loud, like a good dog. Woof! Woof! Woo-hoo! Woo-hoo!'

He looked straight at me, although I didn't believe he could see me. He seemed to be unsure if he had heard anything at all and, thus, didn't want to make a fool of himself. I grew impatient.

'You stupid mutt! Bark like you're supposed to. You're a bloody dog, aren't you? You fool!'

He actually growled and quite possibly cursed at me in doggy language as he sounded out a torrent of outraged barking. The light of the torch swept over us instantly. I dived at the dog again and this time he tried to get at me, pushing at Jim with his sharp claws as he thought to clamber up on to his chest. This roused Jim slightly and he coughed just a little but the small bubble-shaped cloud that appeared in front of his mouth was enough. The officer yelled out excitedly, 'Over there. Look over there. There's a live one. Hurry up, boys!'

His men didn't delay and they crossed over to Jim in a miraculous amount of time. The senior officer stretched out to hoist him in. 'You're alright, mate. We've got you. You're safe now.' They wrapped him in someone's coat, one of the men even removing his own jacket to put around Jim's head. When they were satisfied that he was breathing a little more regularly, they turned out to the ocean again, to see if there was anyone else they could save.

'What about the dog, sir?'

Alas, the dog had used up all his energy with that bout of angry barking. Once he stopped swimming, the cold, icy water made short work of him, slowing down his heart and sending him to sleep, during the few minutes the men worked to revive Jim. I had hoped he'd make it. He certainly deserved to.

'I'm afraid he's a goner, poor thing. This chap has a lot to thank him for.'

There was no one else in need of their help, so they headed off in the direction of the other lifeboats. I stayed by the dog and watched them go, elated over the fact that I had accomplished my self-appointed mission. Jim was safe. Isobel still had a husband and her children, a father. My being here had been for something. There had been a reason after all.

'Thank you,' I mouthed, to no one in particular.

⚜ ⚜ ⚜

The silence was incredible after all the havoc. It was eerie. I surveyed the seascape around me. Miles of frozen bodies standing upright in the water, thanks to their lifejackets. There was so many of them, bobbing gently, looking as if they were only sound asleep.

Moving in and around the dead passengers and crew, I hoped I wouldn't see anyone I knew. I couldn't help it; I found myself struck by the beauty of the corpses. There was a girl of maybe ten or more. Her skin shone in the night light while the drops of ice that were fixed to her cheeks sparkled like diamonds. She had been captured in a perfection that would never be smudged by pimples or wrinkles. A baby boy floated by, his face and hand as blue as his blankets. As I gazed upon him, I was startled by a noise. It wasn't a loud one, more like a gentle 'thud-thud'. Hoping it might be someone else who needed my help, I peered in the direction it was coming from and found myself bitterly disappointed, and sad, to discover it was only a couple of bodies that were bumping up against a small iceberg. The ocean was punctured by icebergs as far as I could make out. They were as silent and still as the dead.

My elation was beginning to disappear. For the first time in a long, long time I was completely alone. I missed them. It was so strange. I hadn't even known them for long – Isobel, Jim, Joseph and Sarah. Their suitcase was at the bottom of the ocean while I was stuck here on top. I also missed *Titanic*, that beautiful ship that I helped to build and made my home. I even ached with loneliness for this dead dog who unintentionally gave his life for another. I missed Uncle Albert, Charlie, Ed, Jack. I missed the stupid boys in my class. And I missed my mother. I only understood now that I had seen something of her in Isobel. But Isobel was gone, busy with her own children, and I was alone in the sea, surrounded by the dead.

The sun started to creep out of its hiding place and I suddenly felt peculiar. I wasn't sure. The air vibrated around me or maybe it was me that trembled. There was something in the air. A softness? A warmth? It was a strange sensation. I was nervous and excited but I didn't know why. Now that was strange; I could smell the breeze. I hadn't been able to smell since my accident. It had a sweet smell as it caressed my face. I could actually feel it. Another thing I hadn't been able to do since the fall. A mist, slightly pinkish in colour, had formed without my noticing it. It stretched out across the ocean and I could no longer see anything except the dog beside me. To my surprise, I heard what sounded like the slapping of a boat upon the water. Had another lifeboat come back to search for survivors?

I had another surprise when I looked down and saw my reflection in the water. Oh my goodness. What was happening? There was my brown hair, my green eyes and even the hint of stubble on my chin. There were my arms and my hands and my legs. My newly-found ears began to throb slightly. The air was buzzing, I was sure of it now. So taken was I with my appearance that I hardly bothered about the approaching boat, if that was what it was. The mist was too thick to see.

'Samuel? Samuel?'

It was a woman's voice, calling my name. How long had it been since I had heard my name said aloud. My face was wet with tears. When did *that* happen? The voice sounded sort of familiar, but I was too dazed to think straight. I stayed where I was. Out of the mist I could make out the shape of a rowing boat, much like the ones on *Titanic*. It sat low in the water and sent ripples towards me long before I could make out two figures. Neither of them appeared to be rowing yet the boat kept coming.

Now a man's voice rang out, 'There he is! Samuel?'

I opened my mouth but I couldn't say anything. I just stared. It was my father, only he looked so much younger than I remembered, dressed in his Sunday suit with his old cap on his head. But how could that be? That cap wasn't with him the night he died. He had left it at home.

'Where is he? Wait, I see him. Oh, my son, my beautiful son.'

I couldn't move. I could only look stupidly back at her. She was beautiful, her hair golden like the sun and her smile utterly radiant as she took my father's arm.

All I could manage were two words, maybe the best two words in the world. 'Ma? Da?'

Before I could attempt to say anything else, something touched my hand. It was the dog, licking me and wagging his tail. I patted him, and felt his curly hair beneath my fingers. It was dry to touch. When I shyly looked back at my parents, I saw that their boat was now one of many. The mist started to lift as the sun climbed higher in the sky. All around me the passengers and crew were being collected by the boats. There were the five postmen, the orchestra with their instruments, Mr Stead, who waved gaily at me, Arthur, the engineers and the bellboys, while Mrs and Mrs Strauss, the elderly couple that wouldn't be parted nor saved, danced their way into their boat.

The Gatti cousins joked in Italian as they fished each other out of the water, and the Swedish family were still holding hands as they were greeted by their long-lost relatives in their boat. Everyone was being met by someone they knew. I saw the man Lucien being embraced by a large, jolly woman that I guessed to be his Aunt Margaret. Next to them was Harry, the foreman, crying over the little boy who called him 'Dada'.

No one was being left behind this time.

Everyone saw me now. I was no longer invisible, no longer alone. Captain Smith, all the little children, Thomas Andrews, Jack Phillips and Doctor O'Loughlin. It was like we had known one another forever. They looked at me expectantly, with smiles of encouragement.

I felt enveloped by love, understanding that love was the warm breeze, the pink mist and the two people that I cared most about. They held out their arms, beckoning me to them.

'Samuel, pet, it's time for you to bring everyone home.'

'Back to Belfast?'

My mother's laughter was instant and light, 'No, my darling, but somewhere just as good.'

Author's Notes

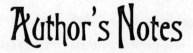

This is a fictional story based on true events. I have included real people, actual dialogue and events as I found them in my research. However, I have taken liberties, here and there, as novelists frequently do.

SAMUEL

Who knows, maybe the ghost of Samuel Joseph Scott did travel with the *Titanic* when she left Belfast two years after his death, but the rest of him is still lying today in an unmarked grave in Belfast City Cemetery (number R-474).

I have 'imagined up' his life story, including his relationship with his parents, for this book, but what I do know for certain is that he was born sometime in 1895 and lived in east Belfast. Because he was only fifteen years old, I would guess that he hadn't been working too long in the Harland & Wolff shipyard before his fatal accident.

Today, in Belfast, Samuel's grave is part of the official tour of the cemetery. His death was the very first tied to the *Titanic*. (Seven others died during the ship's construction and, of course, over 1,500 more would die on the fateful night of the sinking.) The man who runs the tours, ex-Lord Mayor of Belfast, Tom Hartley, wrote a book called *Written in Stone*, which is based on his tour, and this is how I found Samuel ... or he found me.

During the writing of this book I visited the cemetery, and although it was a bit of a disappointment that there was no headstone marking where Samuel lay, it was still a thrill to find myself standing there on 21 April 2010, one hundred years and one day after he died. As I looked around at the other graves, in particular the ones that were older than 1910, it struck me that Samuel's relatives must have been standing in the exact same spot as they prayed for the safe journey of his soul back 'home'.

JIM, ISOBEL, JOSEPH

AND SARAH

Had this family really existed, would they have survived the sinking? As much as I hate to say it, probably not is the answer. Only 178 third-class passengers survived out of a total of 706. This is the actual breakdown:

Third Class men: 75 survived out of 462

Third Class women: 76 survived out of 165

Third Class male children: 13 survived out of 48

Third Class female children: 14 survived out of 31

However, the 76 third-class women that were saved did include sisters, **Maggie and Kate Murphy**, who, thanks to their neighbour **James Farrell**, eventually made it all the way to America where they both found husbands, as Isobel predicted, and had children of their own. Maggie died in 1957, followed by the younger Kate in 1968.

FREDERICK FLEET —

THE LOOKOUT

Frederick survived the sinking, thanks to his being ordered to get into lifeboat 6, but at what price? Unfortunately his colossal guilt, over not seeing the iceberg in time, haunted him for the rest of his life. At the inquiry that followed, Fred insisted that had he had binoculars he could have prevented the disaster. As it was, he never really recovered from the disaster and, at the age of seventy-six, following the death of his wife, he took his own life.

There is a story, whether true or false, about his 'visiting' the American *Titanic* exhibition in Las Vegas. It was said that his ghost lingered around the people who came to see the exhibit, gently touching them as if to reassure himself that they were safe from harm.

His fellow lookout, **Reginald Lee**, also survived, only to die the following year, 6 August 1913, from pneumonia while onboard another ship.

HAROLD BRIDE —

THE TELEGRAPHIST

By the time the *Carpathia* reached the survivors in the life-boats, Harold was suffering from severe frostbite in both his feet. Despite this and his shock over losing his friend, Jack Phillips, he got to work immediately in the ship's telegraph office with Harold Cottam, the *Carpathia*'s telegraphist. As you might imagine, there were at least 700 messages to be sent to worried relatives, assuring them that their loved ones had made it. The two men were exhausted by the time they reached New York, Harold having to be pushed off in a wheelchair on account of his swollen, numb feet.

In later years Harold moved his family to Scotland, to hide out from the limelight that shone permanently on the *Titanic* survivors. He hated talking about the sinking and never got over Jack's death. He died in 1956.

CHARLES JOUGHIN —

CHIEF BAKER

Charles continued to work on other ships after the accident. And we can only assume that he continued to drink whiskey too. He obviously liked America because he made it his home, along with his wife and daughters, dying in 1956, in New Jersey, at the ripe old age of seventy-eight years.

CHARLES HERBERT LIGHTOLLER

— SECOND OFFICER

Lightoller was the most senior officer to survive. His story is possibly the happiest out of all these survivors as he went on to have a very productive career at sea, including taking part in the two world wars. He was only demobbed, or released, from his army duties when he was seventy-two years old. However, instead of relaxing into his retirement, he went on to run a shipyard that built boats for the London River Police. He died in 1952 aged eighty.

JACK PHILLIPS

Perhaps the most controversial liberty I have taken with the *Titanic* story involves the telegraphist Jack Phillips. After finding many conflicting accounts about his last minutes, as to whether or not he made it into the Collapsible boat with Harold Bride, I decided to write my own, but in no way can I take from his achievement. If Jack hadn't bravely stuck by his desk until the very last minute, perhaps the *Carpathia* would never have found those 700 passengers who were freezing in the lifeboats.

ACKNOWLEDGEMENTS

For their invaluable help with this book, I would like to thank: Michael O'Brien for believing in me; my editor Susan Houlden for her passion for the story and advice on the art of writing, and the wonderful designer Emma Byrne.

I also want to thank the brilliant illustrator Dave Hopkins for the cover. The first manuscript was read by three young readers, Jack Newport, Anna Gordon and Tom Moore. They all contributed, with their opinions, to this final draft, and I solemnly thank them for that.

And, finally, thanks to Damian and my family who have had to listen to an awful lot about *Titanic*, especially my dad, who not only drove me to the big exhibition and then had to listen politely as I showed off my research – while trying to enjoy the exhibition himself – but furthermore built me the small model of *Titanic* that I bought in the gift shop.